Mutilated Viking Strippers Take the Pentagon

I0539319

SEAN WALSH

TITLE BY SHAINA KING

COVER ILLUSTRATIONS BY JORDAN WALSH

JORDAN-WALSH.COM

BEWILDERING TALES OF FICTION LOGO BY DAN JAMES

DANJAMESDESIGNCO@GMAIL.COM

COVER LAYOUT BY NANCY RAMOS

NMRDIGITALDESIGN.COM

AUTHOR ILLUSTRATION BY MEGAN PORCH

MEGAN-PORCH.SQUARESPACE.COM

For Rose.

I will love you until the end of time.

And for Rob.

I'm gonna miss you, buddy.

An Introduction

It began simply enough, as I'm sure many things in the social media age have, with a Facebook post. On October 14th, 2014, I posted the following:

"Hello friends!

Please give me a story idea in the form of a title for me to write about. The more ridiculous the better.

Examples: Cannibals of Candyland, Satan Burger, Ultrafuckers. Sadly, these are all taken.

Thanks in advance!"

The results were, unsurprisingly, ridiculous. Of the many responses, I narrowed my selection down to a dozen and the book you hold in your hands is the first release from that collection. The last 2+ years have been a whirlwind creatively and at the time of my writing this introduction, nine of the twelve are finished to some degree. The other three are in some form of completion, and a handful of other stories outside of the project have been written in the time between that post and now.

My friend Shaina, who I've known since elementary school, suggested many titles but the one that really struck me was *Mutilated Viking Strippers Take the Pentagon*. More than most of the titles I selected to spin into short stories, its name informed the plot. I just needed to figure out where exactly these mutilated Viking strippers were coming from. Around the time I was thinking of zombified exotic dancers in Vikings jerseys, I realized I was looking a little too closely at the problem. I stepped back and thought to myself: why can't they just come from another dimension?

Then, some time later, while playing *Rogue Legacy* (a love letter to the *Castlevania* franchise), I thought to myself "Damn, I wanna write a

Castlevania-inspired character but I already have my hands full with these stories, I shouldn't be starting more." Then I realized I already had the Lich as my main antagonist so why not swap Dracula out with him and create my very own Belmont family? Thus Marjorie Lenoir was born.

Then, one Monday morning after a particularly fruitful Sunday of working on *Mutilated Viking Strippers*, I realized how influenced by author Brian Keene's style the story was and decided to tweet him as such.

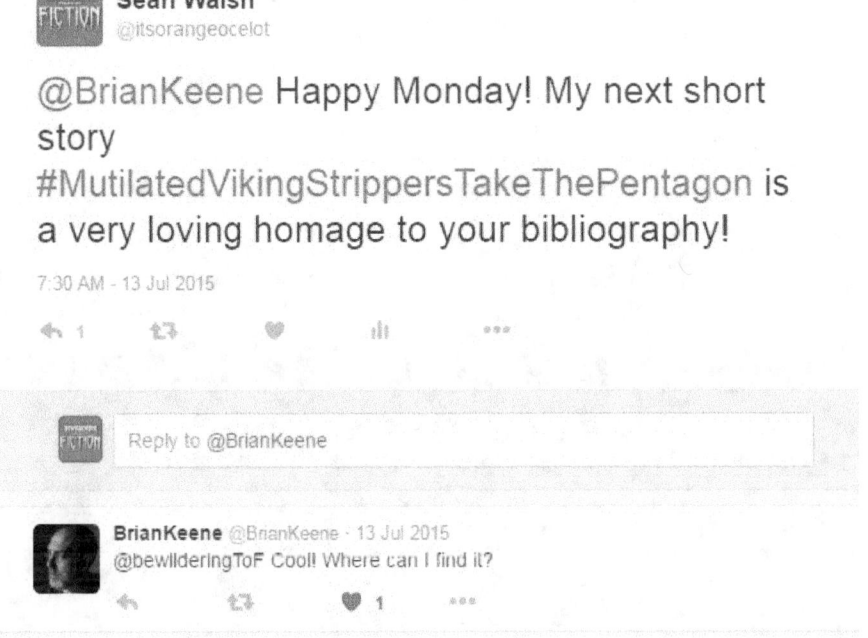

Sean Walsh
@itsorangeocelot

@BrianKeene Happy Monday! My next short story #MutilatedVikingStrippersTakeThePentagon is a very loving homage to your bibliography!

7:30 AM - 13 Jul 2015

Reply to @BrianKeene

BrianKeene @BrianKeene · 13 Jul 2015
@bewilderingToF Cool! Where can I find it?

Upon his response, I decided that I *had* to publish it so I could send him a hardcopy. It was still some time before I finished it (clearly) but now here we are. So if you're reading this, Brian, thank you for the motivation.

I am very proud of this story and I am so grateful for everybody that has helped in some form or another with the finished product: Dan James, for the awesome pulp-influenced banner on the cover, my brother Jordan for the incredible cover illustration and character designs, my proofreaders, everybody who gave me feedback over the lengthy process of making this book a reality, and every single one of you holding this book in your hands. All of y'all are the real MVPs. There's a much lengthier list of thank yous in the back, I promise.

Now, let's get on with the show!

Act One:
Bring Your Daughter to Work Day

I.

Marjorie Isabella Lenoir stood before the entrance of the Lich's castle. Now that she was in front of it, the lair was even more imposing. The young woman was on a mission to find the Lich's phylactery and destroy it, finally ridding her kingdom, nay, her entire realm of the Lich's evil.

A trembling hand rested on the hilt of Finem. The enchanted blade was the only thing she had to remember her father by. There was an incredible sense of foreboding emanating from the stone monstrosity before her. The castle was sure to be brimming with all kinds of nasty creatures, and Marjorie could only hope that all her training would get her through the trial that stood before her.

Her father and her three brothers, all famed monster hunters, had fallen before the Lich. She was the last of the Lenoirs, and that meant it was up to her to slay the undead bastard once and for all.

"It's okay to be afraid, child," a disembodied voice assured.

"I'm not afraid," she said to the voice. "Just...apprehensive. Slaying zombies in the graveyard is one thing. I'm sure whatever is beyond those doors is much, much worse."

"I believe in you, Marjorie. I'm sure that your father and brothers are watching from above, cheering you on."

The voice belonged to the original owner of the sword, Arthur d'Argetan. Through a ritual, his essence had been transferred to the sword upon his death, and whomever wielded the sword could communicate with him telepathically.

Marjorie's father found Finem in the keep of a vampire lord he'd slayed. He would've completely overlooked the weapon had d'Argetan not called out to him. Finem quickly became his preferred weapon, and after receiving the holy blessings of the Monks of the Divine Order, it cut through evil like a hot knife through butter.

D'Argetan was kind, thoughtful, and most importantly, knowledgeable; he provided a comforting voice in a dark, dreary world. With Finem around, Marjorie felt a little less alone.

"Well, what're we waiting for then?" d'Argetan asked.

Marjorie drew the blade. "Right then. Let's kill us a Lich."

She entered the castle.

II.

When the electronic wind chimes he'd set as an alarm began going off on Jefferson Brody's cell phone, the man emitted a lengthy, pained groan. The normally-soothing sound of the chimes may as well have been explosions to the hungover man. Rolling over, he grabbed the phone, shut off the alarm and looked at the time. It was 6:00 on a Friday. Almost the weekend.

There was a text message waiting for him from his ex-wife, Frannie. It read "Don't forget that it's Bring Your Daughter to Work Day, asshole." Jefferson and Frannie's relationship had become rather antagonistic since their divorce.

Jefferson heard a sleepy murmur from the right side of the bed. He turned over and saw a blond woman lying there, mostly asleep.

"Fuck," he said to himself quietly, sliding a hand down his stubbly face. He'd forgotten all about her. The night before, Jefferson had gone out with a couple of the guys from work and found himself taking advantage of The Bar of the Unknown Soldier's five-for-five special on Jell-O shots. After ingesting far too many of the deceptively-strong treats, the blond, whose name he couldn't quite place --*Dora? No, that didn't sound right*-- sidled up next to him and asked if he'd like to buy her a drink. After that things got kind of hazy. Jefferson remembered enjoying himself, and he'd gotten home safe with his lady friend in tow, but that was about it.

Letting the woman --*Debbie, maybe?*-- sleep, Jefferson dragged himself into the bathroom. He turned on the shower and looked at himself in the mirror. He flexed, always appreciative of the chiseled-by-the-gods frame he'd forged out of the chubby body he'd had all through middle and high school. A lot of work had gone into his body, and it paid off on a regular basis; Debbie --*Dottie? No, that's not a name anymore*-- being a prime example of that. One thing he did remember from the previous evening was when she told him he looked just like Channing Tatum. He grinned at his reflection. She was definitely not wrong.

As he showered, Jefferson thought about his new station in life. He worked for the Department of Defense's Social Media department. It was supposed to be a punishment, after having made one too many jokes about his NSA superiors' Internet history, but getting paid $60,000 a year to maintain the DoD's Twitter feed, Facebook page, and Pinterest (he still wasn't exactly sure how Pinterest worked, but he kept pinning pictures of cats dressed in little Armed Forces uniforms and people seemed to really enjoy that) suited Jefferson's laid-back life-style just fine. He'd been doing the job for a month and had already doubled their Twitter followers. It was easy, low-maintenance, and nobody cared if he came in hung over.

"Want some company?" the blond from the previous night asked, stirring him from his thoughts.

Jefferson turned to her to see she was very naked. "Oh, uh, I have to get ready for work."

"I'll work fast, then," she said with a grin, stepping into the shower.

How could he say no to that?

III.

Jack Manning was awake before his alarm went off. He didn't sleep much, not since Bethany and the girls…

The sharp drone of his alarm clock began. Jack wiped his teary eyes and turned the alarm off. Time to begin another day, same as the rest. He didn't know what kept him going. It certainly wasn't his job, and he had no friends or family, not anymore. All the same, he dragged his aching body out of bed and into the shower.

For breakfast, Jack pulled a ham and cheese Hot Pocket out of the freezer, tossed it in the microwave, and poured himself a cold cup of yesterday's coffee. Walking out the door, he bit into the cold-on-the-outside, scalding-on-the-inside turnover and thought about what his shrink had said.

She'd told him he needed to find some closure; pack up the girls' room, sell the house, start fresh.

As he drove to work, Jack thought that putting things in boxes wasn't going to give him closure.

Only revenge would give him closure.

IV.

If there was one thing that Senator Laura Powers (R-Texas) hated more than the liberal media, it was traffic. She sat in her black 2015 Honda Accord and scowled, Frank Sinatra's croon from her car stereo doing little to ease her frustration.

She had been in town on business and ended up getting sucked into helping some fresh-faced grad student make their deadline on some project or another at the Department of Immigration Studies. The Senator had the unenviable job of heading up that particularly obscure department of the United States government. It was a largely thankless job but that was probably for the best. The less the public knew about the DIS and her involvement with it, the better.

Sinatra gave way to a smooth jazz instrumental she didn't recognize. The Senator was too busy grinding her teeth as the rows of traffic slowly crawled along to care. If she was lucky, she'd make the Pentagon by lunchtime. The grad student with the thesis needed some ancient documents that were so old they weren't even worth being scanned. Laura Powers had been a goddamn state senator since the girl's parents were in diapers for Christ's sake and yet here she was, driving to the Pentagon at 8:30 in the morning to dig around in some forgotten tomb full of papers so old they'd make that socialist grump Sanders look like one of those kids on the Disney Channel.

As soon as she was done at the Pentagon, the Senator promised herself that she would get someone to move the documents over to the DIS and scanned into their database. It was 2016 for fuck's sake, there was no excuse for that to not have happened a goddamn decade ago.

Someone behind her blared their horn and Senator Powers gripped her steering wheel so hard her knuckles turned white. *That grad student had better win a goddamn Nobel Peace Prize someday*, she thought to herself.

V.

Jefferson pulled up to Frannie's house an hour later. Before he could knock, she opened the door and stepped outside. His ex-wife was as beautiful as ever, practically a carbon copy of Maggie Grace, all blond hair and legs that stretched up to the heavens. She was wearing a bright neon green spandex top and matching black pants. Jefferson guessed she was going to be running off her frustration shortly after he took their daughter for the day. He tried not to let his eyes linger on the skin-tight fabric clinging to her slender frame.

"You look hung over," she said, stirring him from his surveillance and beginning their requisite argument in record time.

Jefferson nodded and grinned. "So what if I am?"

Frannie scowled at him. "If June wasn't looking so forward to this, I'd tell you to go fuck yourself. Showing up here hung over. Unfuckingbelievable," she growled. "I'm genuinely surprised you don't still reek of alcohol."

Jefferson sighed and pinched the bridge of his nose. "Frannie, can we not do this? Your shrill voice is like a jackhammer to my brain right now."

"Good!" she said loudly.

Jefferson winced.

The door opened and June walked out, a beautiful little doppelganger of her mother with his dark hair. "Dad!" she yelled as she threw her arms around his waist in a bear hug.

Jefferson hugged her back. "Hey, Princess," he said, smugly grinning at Frannie. "You ready to go to the Pentagon?"

June looked up at him with a 1000-watt smile. "I sure am!"

"Good! Now, go get in the car. Your mother and I need to talk. Adult stuff."

June playfully rolled her eyes. "I'm going, I'm going…"

"You're an asshole," Frannie hissed once June was out of earshot.

"Why, Frannie? Because I allow myself to enjoy my life instead of living like a hermit?" He grinned again. Needling his ex was one of his favorite pastimes. "Let me ask you something: When's the last time you got laid? That could explain your demeanor."

Frannie's face wrinkled with anger. "I do *not* live like a hermit! I do hot yoga twice a week and if you must know, I've started seeing a very handsome doctor. And not that it's any business of yours, but he makes house calls three times a week, *thank you very much*."

Jefferson's grin only widened. "So you're this unpleasant for no reason, then?"

She shot him a death glare in response. "Get the fuck off my property, Jefferson."

"Your wish is my command, Your Majesty," Jefferson said, bowing.

He walked down the walkway to his car, then turned around. "You should reap the benefits of dating a doctor. He might be able to prescribe something for that mean case of Bitchy Resting Face you have."

Frannie gave him the finger and went back inside.

As he got into his car, Jefferson couldn't help but smile.

15

VI.

Tammy McElroy was early, as she so often was, to work. As Assistant Manager of the Ground Zero Cafe, she made it her mission to look as eager to work as possible. It's not that she loved her job, in fact she hated it, but she was in a tremendous amount of debt due to a bad investment and a worse addiction. Giving her shit-heel brother Shane $20,000 for his Internet start-up turned out to be almost as big a failure as their little sister Pamela's gluten-free cupcake shop. Speaking of failures, Tammy had a rather debilitating habit of betting on horses. At least, Tammy rationalized as she wiped down the back counter, she'd had the self-control to not seek out a loan shark or take out a second mortgage.

John, the GZC manager, was older than dirt and he hated his job at least as much as Tammy hated hers. It was Tammy's mission to get as many brownie points as possible so that when he retired in what she hoped would be a scant several months (his granddaughter was expecting her first baby and Tammy was really counting on John retiring to spend what fleeting time he had left with the little tyke), that she would be the one to get the pay raise, the back office, and the power to delegate all the stuff she hated to do to whomever she chose as the new Assistant Manager. Probably Gil, because he was both a hard worker and would likely shine her shoes with his tongue if she were to ask.

He'd probably enjoy it too, she thought, smirking. And who could blame him? She checked herself out in the mirror behind the counter. At forty-nine, Tammy thought that objectively, she was still a fox. She had always been thin and despite the extra weight she'd put on since her metabolism had tapered off, the Spanx kept everything in its proper place. Since going into debt, she'd had to start doing her own dye-jobs but she thought the result was actually pretty good. You'd never know there were grays mixed in with that straw-colored farm girl blond hair. *Yeah,* she thought, *I still got it.*

16

Having finished wiping down the countertops and as well as reassuring herself that she was still sexually desirable, Tammy got the coffee pots percolating and prepared for another totally average day of tedium.

VII.

Between d'Argetan's sage advice when it came to monster hunting, Finem's impossibly sharp blade and holy enchantments, and the various weapons Marjorie couldn't go two rooms without stumbling upon, the apprehension and fear were quickly dissipating. Instead, she found herself growing more and more confident with every monster she sent back to the netherworld.

As she collected the gold left behind by the enormous three-headed hellhound she had just slain, d'Argetan spoke up. "Don't allow your newfound confidence to get the best of you. I have seen it happen to more experienced monster hunters than you, including Jasper."

Marjorie thought of her brother Jasper. All the Lich sent back to them was an urn full of ashes. He had been the last of her brothers to fall. She was the only one left, and it was up to her to destroy the Lich and free her realm of his evil. "I won't, d'Argetan. You don't need to worry about me."

"All I *do* is worry, girl. I don't exactly relish the thought of spending another half-century in some monster's treasure room."

She rolled her eyes. "I never knew you cared."

"You know I do, Marjorie. Now, with the Cerberus dealt with, all that remains before we'll be able to enter the Lich's chamber is to slay the Demogorgon and the Dreadnought."

Marjorie smiled. She couldn't help herself. With each monster she disposed of, she felt closer and closer to her father and brothers. She was becoming every bit the monster hunter they had been. "Let's do this."

VIII.

"Those no-good high school dropout needle-dick *idiots* forgot my goddamn Habanero Ranch!" General Albert Wyngarde growled to himself in his car in the parking lot of the Pentagon.

Not only did he have to spend his Friday playing nursemaid to the good little boys and girls of the Department of Defense, he now had to start his day with two Egg McMuffins sans Habanero goddamn Ranch sauce!

The General was less than thrilled to spend the last day before his weekend sitting in an office that wasn't his and twiddling his thumbs while staring at the clock until whoever was going to be relieving him turned up.

If Wyngarde ever found the suit who decided it was a good idea to take all but a skeleton crew of soldiers from their posts for some new anti-terrorism training exercises, he'd show that son of a bitch just how he felt about them and it would *not* be pretty. But orders were orders and just like all the men and women who served beneath him, the shit rolled downhill from the top and Albert Wyngarde found himself with the unenviable task of making sure that nothing bad happened to the folks at the Department of Defense.

The worst part of it was that he knew, *knew*, that they would stick him with a bunch of wet behind-the-ears kids that didn't know a gun barrel from a fucking *Donkey Kong* barrel.

Taking a bite of his first Egg McMuffin (Ruby, God rest her soul, would rise from her grave and choke him to death if he got any of the stuff those jokers passed off as meat on top of his egg discus), Wyngarde tried the breathing techniques that his son-in-law, the shrink, had taught him. It wasn't working, so he opted for plan B.

19

Plan B involved thinking about the weekend he had planned. As soon as he was released from babysitting, the General was driving down to Virginia Beach to spend the weekend with his son and daughter and their collective four children, all of whom were the apples of Wyngarde's eyes. His daughter Tracy (the one married to the head doctor) had two girls: Janey, a 25-year-old law student, and Lisa, and 20-year-old poetry major. His son Robert and his wife Carla, on the other hand, had produced two boys: Robert Jr., a 22-year-old recovered addict and motivational speaker who went around to high schools and told his story, and Martin, their 20-year-old adopted son from Rwanda, an illustration major at an art school up in Beverly, Massachusetts.

Although Wyngarde would never admit it, Martin was his favorite. The kid was big into comic books and fantasy novels and his enthusiasm for both was contagious. Ninety-nine times out of a hundred, he lost Wyngarde almost out of the gate, but Wyngarde didn't care. He just liked to hear the kid talk about the stuff he loved. The two had special plans for their weekend getaway to abscond to the local movie theater to see a screening of that Val Kilmer movie from the 80's where he protects the baby with that little person from *Leprechaun*. *Willow?* The General nodded to himself. That sounded right.

Knowing he was just over eight hours away from hanging out with his grandkids went a long way to restoring the General's mood and as he finished his second McMuffin, he felt ready to face the long, boring day ahead of him.

At least he'd have time to get some reading done, he thought to himself as he got out of the car. Martin had given him a book called *Heart-Shaped Box* by Stephen King's son Joe Hill for Father's Day and despite the fact that the protagonist was one of those long-haired Alice Cooper types, Wyngarde found it surprisingly to his liking.

He always did love a good horror story.

IX.

"...and here is where the magic happens," Jefferson said, opening the door to the Social Media department.

His daughter, named after the month she had been conceived, looked at the small converted janitor's closet. There were two desks, two chairs, two computers, several (empty) filing cabinets, and a framed picture of the President on the wall. "It's...kind of small," June said. Jefferson knew she was trying to be nice.

"Well, as boys will go on to tell you many times as you grow older, it's not the size that counts."

June groaned. "Gross, dad."

"Sorry," Jefferson said, trying to hide a grin.

"So, what do you do all day?"

Jefferson sat down at his desk, turned on his computer, and spun his chair around to face his daughter. "I basically look for interesting things to post about the Department of Defense on Facebook, Twitter, et cetera."

June nodded. "I see. Didn't you used to spy on people?"

He grinned. "Sort of. Mostly on my superiors. They didn't like that much, which is why I'm here in this tiny room posting pictures of cats in sailor suits."

June's face lit up. "That sounds *adorable*! Can I see?" She sat down in the other chair and wheeled it over to where Jefferson was sitting.

21

"Sure thing. I've got a whole folder of them. Just have to wait for the computer to start up."

"Why is there a little girl in my seat?" a gruff voice asked.

Father and daughter turned to see a bald man with his sour disposition plastered to his face standing in the doorway, holding a coffee cup that proclaimed "#1 Dad."

"I'm not *little*, I'm eleven."

"June, this is my co-worker, Gramps. Gramps, this is my daughter, June."

The older man glared at Jefferson, then looked at June. "My name is not 'Gramps,' it's Jack, Jack Manning."

"'Bond, James Bond,'" June said in a low voice. She then launched into a fit of giggles.

Jack looked at Jefferson. "*Cute kid*," he said, his voice icy.

Jefferson stood up. "June, you stay here with Gramps and I'll go get you another chair."

"Okay. Make sure it has wheels!" she said, spinning in Jack's chair.

As Jefferson passed Jack, the man said, "Don't be long. I'm...not good with kids." He stared into his mug and added, "Not anymore."

"Roger that, Jack."

X.

Art Spiegel, Principal Deputy Assistant Secretary of Defense for Energy, Installations, and Environment, was severely constipated. He had meant to stop at the pharmacy on the way to work and pick up some laxatives but the sheer agony of not being able to move his bowels was all-consuming and he drove right past not one, not two, but *all three* Rite-Aids on his morning commute. He'd already used up all of his sick days for the year a few months earlier when he came down with a nasty case of food poisoning from some undercooked pork he'd made himself when Irene had gone on her business trip to Reno.

The thought of selling his soul to cure his constipation had crossed Art's mind innumerable times over the past two days, but just two weeks earlier he'd read *The Monkey's Paw* on a whim. Even if deals with the devil weren't works of fiction, the end result would probably have him endlessly shitting himself until he was dead. Faustian deals were never worth it and so there he was, playing match-three games on his phone and desperately trying to move his bowels.

At least he was getting paid for it.

XI.

Jack wasn't lying when he said he wasn't good with kids. He and the girl sat across from each other in an awkward silence so thick that you'd need a SWAT team to breach it.

Finally, the girl tried to break the silence. "So, do you have kids?"

Jack found himself startled. "W-why would you ask that?"

She pointed at Jack's mug. "Your cup says #1 Dad."

He looked at his coffee mug. He had forgotten what it said on it. "Huh. Yeah. Well, no. Not anymore."

"What happened?"

The kid was a precocious little shit. Something Jack presumed came from her father. Despite all the grief he gave Jefferson, and the reciprocal grief he was given, he liked the guy most of the time. Jefferson reminded him of himself before he became so bitter and jaded, long before the girls were

"They died," he answered. He wasn't going any deeper into than that.

Then, the girl did something that took Jack by complete surprise. She stood, crossed the small room, and hugged him. He didn't know how to react, so he just sat there and let her hug him.

"What's going on in here?" Jefferson asked, wheeling in another chair.

"Oh, thank God," Jack said, feeling relief wash over him as the kid released him.

"Did you know Jack had kids but they died, Dad?"

"Yes, June. Now, let's not ever talk about that again, ever. It's kind of a touchy subject. Now, say you're sorry."

The girl looked downright devastated. "Sorry, Jack. I hope you're not mad."

"Naw, kid, it's…it's fine. Don't worry about it."

The expression on the kid's face didn't change.

"Uh, just to show no hard feelings, here." Jack reached into his pocket, pulled out his wallet, and fished a couple dollars out of it, and handed it to her. "Why don't you go buy yourself a candy bar or a soda or something?"

The girl's whole face lit up. "Ooh, Dad, can I?"

"Sure, hon. Just take a right and go all the way down to the end of the hall. You'll see the break room, there's a couple vending machines in there. Just come right back."

"Okay!" she said, snatching the two dollars from Jack's hand.

Once the girl left the room, Jefferson grinned at Jack. "I had no clue you had such a soft spot, Gramps."

"Fuck you, Jefferson," Jack muttered. "You owe me two bucks."

"There's my guy!" the younger man said.

Jack grumbled to himself as he turned back to his computer.

XII.

While Jefferson had gone in search of a chair for June, he thought about poor Jack and how hard it must be for him on a day like Bring Your Daughter to Work Day. They never talked about it, but everyone in the building knew his story. Jack had been an agent for the CIA, investigating the company Roosevelt Global Solutions and its CEO, Archimedes Roosevelt II. The company was under suspicion of, among other things, illegal genetic research, unsanctioned weapon development, and kidnapping. Coming home one morning after a long night of staking out Roosevelt Global's Maryland branch, Jack found his wife and two young daughters had been brutally murdered. The cops said it had been the Chinese Triad sending Jack a message, something to do with a years-old case. Jack had been completely destroyed, spiraling into a deep, nearly suicidal depression. When he finally came back to work, the man was unhinged; drinking on the job, brutalizing suspects during interrogations, and, so the story goes, picking off members of the Triad in his free time. That last part probably wasn't true, but Jefferson certainly wasn't going to be the one to ask. Jack was bounced around for a while, getting bumped lower and lower down the ladder, until they winded up sticking him in a tiny room with a computer and minimal interaction with the outside world.

Naturally, Jack was less than thrilled when Jefferson had started, but the two had managed to find a way to coexist with minimal antagonism. Jefferson stayed out of Jack's way and Jack stayed out of Jefferson's. Jefferson did take pleasure in the occasional needling of the other man, but only because he was trying to get the guy to lighten up.

Jefferson knocked on the door to the Human Resources department. The cute dark-haired HR woman, Alex, looked up and smiled when she saw him.

"Hey lady, what's the haps?" Jefferson liked Alex. She had the shy nerd with chic glasses and cardigan thing going on, like some kind of sexy librarian. The Cardigan of the Day was a fuzzy pink number that stretched across her sizable...qualifications just right.

Alex shrugged. "Oh, you know, nothing much. Just desperate for 5:00."

"But the day just started!"

The woman rolled her eyes. "I *know*, but they blocked streaming media here so now I can't watch *Puella Magi Madoka Magica* at work, the jerks."

"Those motherfuckers," Jefferson said, grinning. "Say, do you think I could borrow a chair? My daughter's here as part of Bring Your Daughter to Work Day and me and Gramps only have the two in our office."

"Of course!" Alex stood and walked across the small office to an empty desk. As she grabbed the chair, she paused. "Hey, uh, Jefferson? I just remembered something."

"What's up?"

"Bring Your Daughter to Work Day was canceled. Did you not get the e-mail?"

Jefferson sighed. "C'mon, you can't expect me to read every e-mail I get. Do you read all of yours?"

"Ha!" Alex said with a grin. "Of course not." She brought the chair over to Jefferson. "Here's the chair. You'll have to bring your daughter by, I'd love to meet her."

"Sure thing. Good luck with getting through the day without anime, Alex."

She shrugged. "I'll make it through somehow. I'll just have to bring my DVDs in tomorrow."

"That'll show the suits upstairs. Catch you later, Alex," Jefferson said as he made his way back to the Social Media department.

XIII.

SHUNK!

With one final blow, Finem was lodged deep into the remaining head of the Demogorgon. The horrible demon-spawn had two heads (one of which Marjorie had generously removed for it), four tentacle arms, and a ferocious speed unlike anything she'd encountered previously.

As the monster fell to the ground and bags of gold sprung forth from its body, Marjorie found herself out of breath. The fights were getting harder, but she still emerged victorious. A couple chicken legs, a mana potion, and a trip to a Save Room and she would be back on her feet and ready to take on the Dreadnought.

After collecting all the gold from the fallen hell lord, Marjorie checked her magic map. It auto-filled as she got deeper and deeper into the Lich's castle, which was incredibly handy considering the enormity of the structure. The closest Save Room, conveniently, was right across the hallway from the room she stood in.

As she made her way out of the room, there was a massive rumbling from high above.

"Something's happening," she said.

"Then we better hurry. The Dreadnought is the last of the beasts before we can face the Lich and end his reign of terror before he unleashes whatever horrors he has up his ancient, evil sleeves," d'Argetan told her with urgency.

Marjorie quickened her pace as she made her way to the Save Room.

XIV.

Roger Watts, corpulent financial management analyst for the United States Armed Forces, stood in the break room in front of the candy and soda vending machines. He was torn. He only had enough money for a candy *or* a soda but he really wanted both. He held his last dollar in one meaty paw and the quarter he'd found on the men's room floor clutched in the other as he stood before the vending machines.

The guy from the vending machine company came on Thursdays and that meant both machines were full up, which did not help his choice in the slightest. Pouring over every delectable item behind the glass window of the candy machine, Roger wished someone else was there to make the choice for him.

A little girl walked up, stuck two dollars into the soda machine, and pressed the button for Diet Coke.

The vending machine rumbled as the can made its way down the machine's hidden passages. While she waited, the girl looked up at Roger's portly form and smiled. "Hello!"

"Hi," he said, smiling back. She reminded him of his niece. The same niece his sister would use against him when it came to his eating habits. 'Do you want to die before you get to see that little girl graduate from high school? From *middle school*?' she'd ask him during one of her routine lectures. Angela didn't understand his addiction, nor did she try to.

Maybe this little girl was a sign. He watched as she picked up the can of Diet Coke, popped the tab, and took a big long swig. "Ahhhhhh," she sighed, obviously delighted by the chemical sweeteners doing their job. But did he really want to start his diet on a Friday? Or did he want a four-pack of Oreos? Why was life so hard?

The girl sat down at a table in the empty break room and watched him. Feeling her eyes on him was not helping Roger's decision-making.

Trying to ignore her, he focused at the task at hand.

XV.

A chirp came from Jefferson's pocket. He pulled out his phone and saw that he had a text from a number he didn't recognize. It read "can't wait to see u again mr. pentagon" followed by a Hand Pointing emoji and a Hand Doing the A-OK Sign emoji, the universal emoji pairing for sex.

He grinned but didn't reply. It was best to let them dangle a little bit, lest they become clingy. He saved her number in his phone as "Dora or Debbie(?)" and decided that he'd respond back after dropping off June at Her Royal Bitchiness's house.

Despite himself, Jefferson found his thoughts drifting to Frannie. The two of them lasted far longer than any of their friends thought they would. June was a big part of that, but there was a magnetism between the two adults that was almost impossible to deny. Even that morning as she was giving him a hard time, he found himself undressing her with his eyes and he'd like to think, as the male ego is an incredibly fragile instrument, that she may have at least undone a button or two on his shirt in her head.

Nobody would've believed him had he told them it hadn't been him who had done the cheating. Jefferson Brody was a compulsive flirt and always had been. But he had never strayed. It was Frannie who had been caught by him in their bed with another man. Jefferson chose to take the blame for the sudden implosion in their marriage because he knew that Frannie couldn't handle June thinking that she was the bad guy. June was always Daddy's Girl and, as both parents had suspected, not even Daddy ruining their marriage could drive a wedge. But if it had been Frannie...just the possibility that their daughter would want nothing to do with her if she knew the truth nearly caused her to break down on more than one occasion.

Jefferson knew it was guilt that drove Frannie's antagonism. She hated herself for making him the monster and hated him for letting her. Despite all of the shit that rained down upon him in the wake of the news that they were splitting up, Jefferson still loved Frannie if for nothing else than for delivering unto him their beautiful baby girl. No matter what happened between the two of them, he still got to see his little lady every other weekend and on special occasions like Bring-Your-Daughter-to-Work Day, even if he knew full well that said special occasion *had* been canceled. Jefferson wasn't going to let a little thing like that stop him from seeing June.

His only real regret was letting Frannie take primary custody. He knew he had to play the part of the fuck-up and he played it well, but every time he had to drop the kid off at her mother's place a little part of him died inside. Maybe when he dropped her off that night, he'd broach the subject of renegotiating their terms...

"Are you going to just listlessly stare at your phone all day or do you think maybe you'll actually get around to doing the job you're paid far too much for at some point?" Jack asked him.

Jefferson looked at the older man and jumped to his feet, standing at attention. "Yes sir, Gramps, sir! Next stop: Buzzfeed's Top 20 Cats Dressed as Members of the Armed Forces!" He saluted the man, sat back down, and turned to his computer.

Jack mumbled something to himself and Jefferson couldn't help but grin.

MUTILATED VIKING STRIPPERS TAKE THE PENTAGON

XVI.

Winona Wagner was taking an early break, eating a Greek yogurt in the Pentagon's central courtyard. Her job of a data analyst just wasn't thrilling her the way it used to and she wasn't sure how much longer she could keep it up. It wasn't the location, it wasn't the people and it certainly wasn't the pay; it was the work itself. It was just so fucking *boring*.

As she brought another spoonful of Pomegranate yogurt to her lips, Winona resolved to call her sister Wendy (their parents, Wayne and Whitney, loved alliteration) that night and ask her if she had a spot for her at the used book store.

Nodding to herself, Winona was off in her own little world, picturing what it would be like to spend eight hours a day around faintly musty, well-loved novels instead starring at a screen. The daydream distracted her to the point where she didn't notice the bizarre shimmering effect occurring in the empty space several yards away from her.

XVII.

Marjorie threw everything she had at the Dreadnought. It was a colossal, floating mass of bodies that had once been the Lich's followers. They sacrificed themselves in the Lich's name and became the horrid, pulsating monster. As she sliced body after body from the thing, a bizarre steel sphere in the center of it began to reveal itself. It had three lit panels (red, yellow, and green) and emitted a monotone hum, both of which puzzled the monster hunter. Once she had a clear shot at it, Marjorie sent a bolt of lightning from her hand and the sphere released a tinny, mechanical howl. Obviously, whatever it was, the sphere was the source of the Dreadnought's power.

Using Finem to dispose of the loose shambling corpses that got too close, she focused on the sphere. After several more bolts, the sphere smoked, its lit panels went out and the humming ceased. The loose corpses all crumpled to the ground and seconds later the ones still attached to the large mass fell to the ground, joining their brethren.

Marjorie stuck around just long enough to pick up the gold the Dreadnought dropped, as well as an amulet. The golden monocle she found, a relic according to d'Argetan, informed her that it would increase her defense against dark energy by five percent. That boon wasn't half as good as the one she gained from the amulet she currently wore, which added five percent holy energy to her blade. Against the Lich, that five percent could make all the difference.

Having slain the last of the guardians, she made haste for the Lich's chambers. The door would finally be unlocked and she could finally avenge her family and free the realm from the undead necromancer and his evil.

It had only been hours, but Marjorie was eons away from the girl she had been when she entered the castle. She was brave, confident, and had tempered the arrogance that she had found herself swept up in due to her early successes, replacing it with a steely resolve that had served her well.

Before long, she stood at the entrance to the Lich's inner chambers. All four stone carvings on the door now glowed an eerie green, symbolizing each slain castle guardian.

"Are you scared?" d'Argetan asked her, sensing the girl's hesitation.

"Yes," she admitted. "Of course I am." Of the Lich, of failing, of meeting her family in the afterlife and seeing the disappointment in their cold, dead eyes.

"Well, that's a good sign. At least you haven't lost your mind yet."

Marjorie smiled and pressed a hand to the cold stone door. She could feel an otherworldly energy emanating from it. "No, not just yet."

Then, she pushed the door open. Somewhere off in the distance, ominous organ music began. It was time to face the final boss.

XVIII.

Meanwhile, here is what all of the characters on our side of the realms were up to just before the proverbial shit hit the fan:

Jefferson scrolled through the results for #wesupportourtroops on Twitter looking for things to retweet, not really paying attention. June had been gone a while, he realized, but how much trouble could the girl really get into in the Pentagon of all places?

Jack was doing largely the same thing as Jefferson, but on Reddit. It was depressing that for every post someone made about the government or the troops that hit the front page, there were ten posts about the goddamn Fruit Fairy. He jotted down a note on a Post-It, reminding himself to 'ask idiot about filtering keywords re: reddit.' Clicking his pen, the man continued scrolling.

June watched the large man with great interest as he deliberated over what to buy from the vending machine. She'd been there five minutes and he was still figuring it out. She had finished her soda but found herself emotionally invested in the man's struggle.

Senator Laura Powers was sifting through a rusty filing cabinet in a dank, dingy, neglected file room well off the beaten path, lamenting that she could've been literally anywhere else. With a quick glance toward the door to make sure nobody was looking, the Senator pulled a flask out of her suit jacket pocket and took a quick swig of vodka. She grimaced as it passed her lips, returned the flask to its hiding space, and returned to the filing cabinet.

General Wyngarde sat in his office-for-the-day and looked at pictures of his grandchildren on his phone. He refused to get a Facebook of his own so he'd made both his son and his daughter promise to send him whatever selfies the kids posted. One that Tracy had sent over that morning of his youngest grandchild, Harmony, showed off a little too much cleavage and when Grandpa was done babysitting the stuffed shirts at the Pentagon, he'd be paying his little princess a visit to talk about her wardrobe.

Alex had shut off her phone's Wi-Fi and relied on 3G (the Pentagon's thick walls sent her back to the digital dark ages before 4G existed) and was patiently waiting for an episode of *One-Punch Man* to load.

Roger still had no idea what he wanted from the vending machine. For a fleeting moment, he had a half-thought about his situation being a metaphor for his whole life, but hunger pangs derailed that train of thought right at the station. There were no survivors.

Tammy, assistant manager of the Ground Zero Cafe, was wiping up a spill. One of the idiots from Finance had knocked over the half-and-half and just left it with a pile of napkins on top of the giant puddle. She shook her head and cursed her stupid brother and his stupid start-up. Why he thought that people would want to spend money on an app that allowed you to collect digital Troll dolls was beyond her, not to mention why she thought investing in it had been a good idea. 'But you can comb their hair!' Shane had insisted. They were both idiots.

Art had begun to weep. He felt like he had to go so bad. He was not a praying man, but he found his hands clasped begging any deity who would listen to help liberate his bowels from the fecal lockdown his body had imposed on them.

Winona had gotten so excited about the idea of working at Wendy's book store that she was going to head straight to HR and put her two weeks in. At the same time as she stood up to do just that, a portal opened up and hell poured through.

Act Two:
Ride of the Valkyrie

I.

When Marjorie entered the Lich's inner sanctum, Marjorie was not sure what to expect. If she had made a list of possibilities of what lay beyond that door, a horde of animated corpses standing in a circle around a skeletal figure in black and red vestments as he read from an ancient tome *probably* wouldn't have been in her top ten.

The Lich didn't seem to notice her and the corpses that surrounded him certainly didn't. It occurred to her that unlike the corpses in the rest of the castle, these ones were just *animated* as opposed to the usual *reanimated* corpses. It was a small but important difference: reanimated corpses acted on their own, shambling around and thirsting for brains while animated corpses were under the control of a necromancer and acted to his will. As the Lich was the most powerful necromancer in the history of Arcania, being able to control a small army of animated corpses would be child's play to him.

But to what end, Marjorie wondered.

She couldn't get a good look at the Lich as his back was to her. She'd never actually seen him before, only heard stories of his horrible, wraith-like visage. Perhaps it was for the best that she hadn't had the chance to see his ghastly form in the flesh yet, as she was already shaking in her boots (the very same boots that allowed her to make a second jump whilst in mid air, a very handy ability when traversing the treacherous labyrinth that was the Lich's castle).

Scanning the room and ignoring the Lich, she looked for his phylactery. It didn't matter how skilled she had become or how many skills and abilities she had acquired; so long as the phylactery remained, so too would the Lich.

Finally, a glass case across the room, beyond the throng of dead women, caught her eye. A brilliant many-angled stone that glowed blood red pulsated within. If that wasn't the phylactery then Marjorie was no Lenoir.

"*Great,*" she whispered to herself, "*now all I have to do is make it all the way across the room, past the most powerful necromancer of all time and his army of lady corpses without being noticed, destroy whatever wards are presumably protecting the case the phylactery is in, and then destroy the phylactery itself. No problem.*"

Before d'Argetan was able to suggest a plan, the Lich finished his incantation. A hole ripped open in reality before her very eyes, bright green energy gathered around it, forming a portal to what appeared to be another world.

"Go, my beautiful Valkyrie!" the Lich croaked with a voice that sound like someone tearing ancient parchment. "Spill forth unto this mundane realm and retrieve that which has been hidden from me for so long." The corpse women followed his instructions and poured through the portal five at a time. Then, he cackled. The sound of his laughter made Marjorie want to heave up the turkey leg she had ingested shortly before her last trip to a Save Room.

Suddenly, to her horror, the Lich turned his attention to her. He was even more horrific than she had imagined, little more than a walking skeleton with strips of leathery skin clinging to his bones. He had green fire for eyes and something told Marjorie that if she kept his gaze for too long, she might never be able to look away.

"Little Marjorie Lenoir, I presume? Your father told me so much about you."

Her hand gripping Finem's hilt but unable to draw the blade, she screamed, "Don't you talk about my father, you monster!"

Even with such little skin left on his face, she could tell that the dread thing smiled at that. "Do you want to know what the last thing he said to me was before I tore his heart from his chest?"

Tears stung Marjorie's eyes but she said nothing. She felt glued to her spot, unable to move, as the Lich drew ever closer.

"He begged for death, just like your brothers after him. It's amazing what a little torture will do to a person. They're all the same in the end, grown men mewling like newborn babes."

The Lich was right in front of her now. A bony finger stroked her cheek. "I wonder if you'll taste as good as they all did."

"*Die, monster,*" Marjorie hissed through gritted teeth. She headbutted the Lich, sending him stumbling, and ran for the phylactery. Raising Finem above her head, a guttural scream ripping forth from somewhere deep within her, Marjorie brought the blade down upon the case. Unfortunately, whatever wards the Lich had placed on it activated, producing a wave of negative energy that sent Marjorie flying backward.

Directly into the portal.

II.

Of the two hundred and seven Department of Defense employees who died that day, Winona Wagner was the first.

The hole in reality appeared with a noise like something heavy hitting the floor from the apartment above you. Winona stared at it, transfixed, as the green wormhole appeared before her eyes. All thoughts of putting in her two weeks, of working at her sister's bookstore, of being spiritually fulfilled, left her mind as she dropped her empty Greek yogurt container on the ground.

"It's beautiful," she said aloud to nobody but herself.

The first corpse woman came through the portal and looked directly at her. It screamed and ran at her, an ax raised above its head.

Winona didn't even have time to respond before the ax blade was buried in her skull, just above her left eye.

Somewhere in her rapidly dwindling consciousness, the woman was vaguely aware as the thing pulled its weapon from her head.

After that, she ceased being aware of anything at all.

III.

Nigel Daniels was eating a bag of Garden Salsa SunChips he'd picked up from the Ground Zero Cafe (a snack, he was proud to say, he'd successfully petitioned for them to add to their selection) while watching the cameras in the central nervous system of the Pentagon. Nothing even remotely interesting had happened since that old cat lady secretary from the Department of the Army got caught stealing office supplies and that was five months earlier.

As he crunched away on his SunChips, something caught Nigel's eye. There was activity at Ground Zero. *A lot of it.*

What appeared to be an army of female corpses dressed like Red Sonja, all chain-mail bikinis and nonsensical bucklers, were hacking people to pieces and storming the interior.

"They're like some sort of...mutilated Viking strippers," Nigel murmured numbly to himself, half a chip falling from his mouth as he stared, transfixed, at the carnage unfolding on the cameras. He'd always thought he'd had a strong stomach as a jaded veteran horror film fan, --having spent the entirety of *The Human Centipede* rolling his eyes and dismissing it as a generic mad scientist film with a really stupid gimmick, for example-- but this...this was *real.*

Grabbing the nearby wastepaper basket, the man deposited the half bag of SunChips he'd eaten as well as what was left of his morning bagel. The splashback from his Garden Salsa-flavored vomit was quite sobering and Nigel realized what he had to do.

Making a cross on his chest, something he hadn't done since he was a kid, he pressed the big red button on the center console, triggering a red alert and locking down the entire facility. Sirens began to sound and the same kind of buzzing as a Severe Storm Warning on TV rang out throughout the facility.

What Nigel failed to realize in his panicked state was while he had at least prevented these monsters from escaping out into the world, he had also managed to trap dozens of his coworkers in with the so-called 'mutilated Viking strippers' that had already managed to infiltrate the building.

Wiping the vomit from his face with one of his sleeves, Nigel sat back down in his seat and watched helplessly as the horror unfolded throughout the facility.

A thought occurred to him: *the carnage was like something out of an Edward Lee book.*

IV.

Senator Powers exited the file room to see what all the fuss was about. There were people running willy-nilly through the halls, looks of fear on their faces. Before she could ask any of them what was going on, a soldier so young he could've practically been one of those child soldiers in Africa ran up to her and saluted.

"Ma'am, you need to come with me," he told her.

"What is going on, young man?"

The boy, pimple-faced and pale, looked at her with wide, scared eyes. "There's been an attack, ma'am. Some sort of zombies."

"Oh...oh my," the Senator stated.

"Please ma'am, we have to get to the bunker."

She gave him a hollow smile and followed him as he led her to the safe room beneath the Pentagon.

V.

When a lockdown is activated in the Pentagon, a signal is sent off-site to an undisclosed location. Upon receipt of the signal, a Navy veteran named Joseph Hunt relays it to the proper channels and they respond appropriately and oftentimes, with great force.

On the day that the Pentagon was invaded by walking corpses, the signal came through like any other time. Joseph, Joe to his friends, picked up the phone to dial a squad of former Green Berets known as the Pentagon Response Team when a message appeared on his monitor.

"FALSE ALARM. DO NOT CONTACT THE PRT."

The message was then followed by a confirmation code that changed daily. The code matched and that suited Joe just fine as the men in the PRT were some *scary* guys. With a shrug, he placed the phone back on its receiver and turned his attention back to his phone and the inane *Hare Trigger* mobile game that his kid had gotten him hooked on, completely oblivious to the carnage that was unfolding on his watch.

VI.

Jefferson nearly fell backward in his chair when the alarms went off. The lights went red and then that horrible pulsing alarm noise began, followed by a woman's voice informing everybody that the facility was under lockdown.

He looked at Jack. "What the fuck is going on?"

Jack, eyes wide, shook his head. "No clue."

Jefferson shot up as he realized, to his great horror, that he had no idea where June was. Jack must've realized the same thing as he was already on his feet.

"Jefferson," Jack said to him, his voice stable.

Jefferson looked at the other man, mouth dry and eyes wide. "What? We have to move *now*."

The older man put his hands on Jefferson's shoulders and looked at him. "Keep it together, okay? The kid doesn't need her dad falling to pieces, alright? Besides, she's in the Department of Defense. She'll be fine."

A smile flickered across Jefferson's lips for a split-second and then he nodded. "Y-you're right," he said, voice wavering. "Thanks, Gramps."

"No problem. Now, let's go find her."

They left the Social Media office, clueless as to what the hell was going on.

VII.

Roger watched as the little girl's eyes flicked around the room. It was obvious she was terrified. He thought of his niece again and knew he had to at least try to comfort the kid.

Ignoring his stomach's cacophony of growls, the fat man approached her. "What's your name, sweetheart?"

"J-June," she stammered.

"Nice to meet you June! I'm Roger."

She starred at him.

Roger squatted, bringing himself down to her level. "You're gonna be okay, hon. I promise."

"I want my dad," she told him with tears in her big, brown eyes.

He nodded. "I know. We'll find him. What's his name, kiddo?"

"J-J-Jefferson Brody."

This took Roger by surprise. He was surprised that a guy like Jefferson had a kid, especially one as old as June appeared to be. Brody was one of those jock-y, good-looking guys, a classic "girls want him, guys want to be him" type. Everybody seemed to love him, especially the ladies, and while Roger didn't have anything in particular against him, the man was undeniably an Adonis. Not exactly high up on Roger's list of people to send a Christmas card to.

"Do you have a cell phone, June?"

She shook her head. "Mom says n-n-not 'til I'm thirteen, which is s-s-stupid because Lisa Eder's the same age as me and h-her mom g-g-got *her* one."

Kids today, Roger thought. "Well, do you know your dad's cell phone number?"

Another head shake. Roger took a deep breath.

"He works in the Social Media department, right?"

At this, at least, she nodded.

"Okay. Let's go get him."

The man held out a large hand and the little girl took it, her much tinier hand swallowed whole by his. They left the break room together, Roger casting one last, forlorn look at the vending machines.

VIII.

Tammy hid in the back office, the door locked and latched. She didn't wait around to find out what was going on, but as soon as she got a look at what was coming out of that portal or wormhole or whatever the hell it was, the woman turned tail and hid. There had been a few customers in the cafe but she was only concerned for her own safety. The banging from the other side of the door was persistent and she knew it would only be a matter of time before whatever was out there got in.

Pulling out her phone, she saw that it was out of service and not connected to the Department of Defense's Wi-Fi or 4G.

Of course.

Hiding under John's desk, the woman began to silently weep. If she hadn't needed the money and the brownie points so badly, she would've told Toni no when the other woman asked her to cover for her so she could go see some band called 'Celebrity Navels.' She would've been at home in bed with her pajamas on, a tub of Roosevelt Farms Bang Bang Banana Fudge Ripple in her lap, binge watching *Parks and Recreation* on Netflix. Instead, she was cowering under the desk of an old man who should've retired years ago, the lingering smell of John's cheap Rite-Aid cologne assaulting her senses, waiting for zombies to find her and eat her brains.

The door to the office finally gave, bursting inward. Tammy stifled a scream and listened as the sound of someone, or something, in bare feet limp-drag its way towards the desk. Fresh, molten tears stung her face. Beneath the sheer terror, a thought occurred that only deepened her despair: she was supposed to go speed dating the following evening with Penelope and Nora.

As the desk was torn away, the woman didn't even look up at her murderer. She just smiled wanly and thought at least she didn't need to worry about that pile of debt she was buried under. It was someone else's problem now.

Tammy barely even felt it as the zombie woman pulled her head back and tore her throat out.

IX.

Alex was terrified. She had done lockdown drills before as part of her training for HR but she'd never actually experienced it for herself. Part of her wanted to barricade the door to the office but a larger part of her knew that she had to help whoever she could.

Steeling herself, the woman pushed her glasses up the bridge of her nose, picked up the gold-plated letter opener from her desk, and left the office.

The hallway was empty, which helped to put her mind at ease, but only a little. She had no idea what was going on but she knew that if an actual lockdown had been initiated it couldn't be good.

White-knuckling the letter opener, she decided to go left towards the break room at the end of the hallway.

X.

"Fuck!" Jefferson screamed at the three-foot thick steel partition that had come down, cutting off the route to the break room. Not only was he separated from his daughter but he didn't know what had caused the lockdown. The uncertainty was maddening.

Jack tapped several different button combinations into the keypad on the partition. After each four-button attempt, it angrily beeped at him.

"I thought the codes might have been the same as when I was in Langley," he informed Jefferson.

"We both know they change those codes like, daily," Jefferson said, a scowl plastered to his usually jovial face.

Jack shrugged. "Kid, we're in this together. Let's save the aggression for whatever it is that put us in this situation in the first place, huh?"

Their conversation was interrupted by several people running from a nearby hallway, a black guy Jefferson didn't recognize and that Asian woman who he was pretty sure worked in the Legal department, Carrie or Cara, maybe? He really needed to work on his name retention.

Jack stopped them. Both were obviously terrified. "What's going on?"

"Fucking zombies, man!" the man screamed.

"This isn't a drill, kid! Be serious!" Jack scolded him.

The woman, her eyes wide with fear, nodded. "He's telling the truth. They came out of nowhere, they're just killing people left and right."

Jefferson looked at Jack, who shook his head ever so slightly. Then, movement caught Jefferson's eye. There were two skeletal women clad in chain-mail bikinis like something out of a hair metal album cover. Whatever said chain-mail was meant for, defense was certainly not at the top of the list. One of the women held a blood-stained sword in the sole hand still attached to her body and the other dragged some sort of giant hammer behind her. Both had ghastly grins plastered to their leathery faces.

"Jesus Titty-fucking Christ," Jack said. "Fucking zombies."

The women approached them at an almost casual pace, like they knew that the four of them were trapped like rats. Carrie or Cara clung to Jefferson and the other man he didn't know had placed himself behind Jack.

"What do we do, Jack?"

The older man reached into his suit jacket and pulled out a Glock. Jefferson was surprised that his co-worker was carrying. With all of the stuff Jack had been through, he wasn't sure that the man should even able to *own* a gun. But, given the circumstances, he pushed the thought out of his head.

"What do we do?" the man asked rhetorically, taking aim at the one-armed zombie with the sword. "What the hell do you think we do, kid?" Then, he fired three bullets into the zombie's skull. He turned to the other one and followed suit. Both of the zombies' heads had been devastated, but they continued their approach.

"I thought you just had to destroy a zombie's brain to stop it," the girl from Legal said quietly.

Jack growled. "Yeah, me too."

"What do we do, Jack?" Jefferson found himself repeating.

The mostly-headless not-zombies were getting close now. Too close for comfort. The girl from Accounting whimpered.

Jack looked at Jefferson and grinned. It was the grin of a man with nothing to lose. "We fight, kid."

Then, he shot out both of the monsters' kneecaps out. They fell to the ground, dropping their weapons, and continued to crawl toward their would-be victims.

Jefferson watched as Jack walked over to where the one-armed one had dropped its sword. He picked up the blade, examined it, and then brought it down on the creature's remaining arm, separating it from the rest of its body. The corpse lay motionless. He followed suit on the other one.

"There," he said, wiping his brow with a sleeve. "That wasn't so hard. Jefferson, you want the hammer?"

Jefferson looked at the unwieldy weapon and shrugged. "Yeah, I guess."

He picked it up with some effort and held it with both hands.

Jack looked at the other two survivors. "How many more are there?"

The man shook his head. "I don't know."

"A lot," the woman answered. "I was at Ground Zero when they came through. I made it back inside just before lockdown. So did some of...them."

Jefferson watched Jack take it all in. After several moments, the man nodded. "Okay. First, we need more weapons. Then, we need to find someone who knows the code for the blast doors. Jefferson here brought his daughter in today and she's on the other side of that hallway," he said, gesturing to the partition behind them.

"Wasn't Bring Your Daughter to Work Day canceled?" the woman asked.

"That's neither here nor there," Jefferson mumbled.

Jack continued: "Once we find the kid, we're going to get her some place safe and then we're going to figure out how to deal with these fucked-up zombies and send them back where they came from. Now, let's go."

"Wait," the woman said.

"What?" Jack snapped.

"I-I'm Cara."

"Tom," the black man informed them. "Wish we had met under better circumstances."

"Yeah, great," Jack said. Then, he headed in the direction where the Cara, Tom and the not-zombies had come from.

After several moments the other three followed behind him, stepping over the writhing, armless corpses.

XI.

Everything had fallen apart in an instant. Marjorie stood, shell-shocked, at the epicenter of the carnage the Lich had unleashed upon this strange, new realm. Everything felt muted; she could tell that most of her relics had become mere trinkets. She raised a hand to fire a lightning bolt at one of the animated corpses as it chased after a woman with skin like ebony only to find that she could barely even summon sparks. The monster hunter could only stare at her hands as the corpse took the woman down to the ground and tore out her throat with its teeth.

Picking up Finem from the ground beside her, she asked d'Argetan what was going on. There was no response. Marjorie felt her shock becoming panic.

"d'Argetan?? Please answer. I don't think I can do this without you."

Nothing.

Fine, Marjorie thought as she wiped tears from her eyes, *I don't need him. They're just animated corpses. Nothing the monster hunter that slew the Dreadnought can't handle.*

She dashed toward the corpse that had killed and partially consumed the poor dark-skinned woman and loosed its head from its body. The wretched thing's body stood and faced her. She pulled back and sliced at its midsection. Despite the fact that all of her magics and enchantments were reduced to near-uselessness, Finem was still the sharpest blade in Arcania and the blade passed straight through the spinal column of the headless wraith and left it halved.

Crushing the thing's skull as she passed it, the last of the Lenoir monster hunters made her way to the next-closest of the corpse-women, the Lich's 'Valkyrie' as he had called them, with designs on leaving it in as many pieces as its sister.

XII.

The chaos he heard from outside of the men's bathroom almost made Art glad that he had been stricken with the worst case of constipation he'd experienced in his life. Whatever was going on out there, why would it spill into that particular bathroom?

All the same, he had found himself perched on top of the toilet seat, pants hastily pulled up, belt still undone. The man could feel his heart pounding in his chest as his leg muscles began to burn from the strain of his position.

The door to the bathroom slammed open. He heard a man screaming, then the sound of a butcher's knife sinking into to a prime cut. The screaming turned to a gurgle and then silence returned.

From his position, Art couldn't see anything but he *knew* that whoever had just killed one of his co-workers was still in the bathroom with him. The only sound aside from his pounding heart was the slow, deliberate footfalls of bare feet on the bathroom's tile floor. The first stall door slammed opened. Then the second. Art liked to have some leg room so he always used the handicapped stall when it was available, so he was all the way at the end.

Stall door after stall door slammed open, the barefoot murderer getting ever closer. The man's horror grew far more severe when he felt his bowels churn. It was like a bad movie, the shit gods finally hearing his praises for sweet release at the worst possible moment. He clenched, trying to hold it in, but between the build-up of the past two days and the abject horror of his impending doom that was no small task.

If he could just get his pants back down around his ankles...

Before Art had the chance to try and liberate his posterior from its khaki prison, the handicapped stall door burst open and a dead woman in some sort of steel bikini stood there, most of her face gone, revealing the skull.

This can't be real, Art thought to himself. As she raised her cleaver, he felt his bowels release. The pain of the blade entering his neck was far more severe than the shame of still being alive as he evacuated his colon. Fortunately for Art, it only took one more strike from the blade to sever his head completely.

If there was any solace in the end for Art Spiegel, it was that when they found his body, they would assume that the act of shitting himself had occurred post-mortem.

XIII.

Roger and June ran into Alex with enough force that the woman's letter opener actually pierced Roger's voluminous gut. Fortunately, due to his bulk, the man barely felt it.

"I'm so sorry!" Alex kept repeating over and over, her make-up running courtesy of the streams of tears springing forth from her pretty brown eyes.

Roger touched the wound. "It's alright, Alex. It even stopped bleeding already. Barely grazed me."

The woman sniffled. "I just feel so *bad*," she said, her watery eyes piercing him far deeper than her letter opener ever could. Like the rest of him, Roger's heart was quite sizable. He was the kind of guy who never forgot a birthday, celebrated Boss's Day, and made sure that the cleaning ladies got a gift basket every Christmas. Seeing Alex so upset made him want to cry as well.

"Not to be rude," June piped up, "but aren't we supposed to be finding my dad?"

The women looked at the girl and Roger could see realization set in. "Are you June?"

The girl nodded.

With a final sniffle, Alex put the accidental stabbing behind her and squatted down to June's level. The fact that her butt crack stood revealed did not escape Roger's notice, but he tried not to stare too long.

"Everything is going to be okay, honey. We'll get you back to your dad lickety-split."

62

Roger couldn't tell if June had registered what Alex said. As far as he could tell, the girl wasn't even paying attention, just staring past the woman. He followed June's gaze and saw what had captured her attention: standing at the end of the hallway, staring at them, was a ghastly creature that looked like a Coffer Corpse from the D&D campaign Roger played every third Saturday of the month. Unlike in the game, this one wasn't represented as a little ruby stone on a campaign map. This one was real, and it was approaching them. He felt June cling to him and whimper. Alex simply stood beside him, silent.

Just then, the fat man had an epiphany: he wanted a King-Size Kit-Kat Bar more than anything in the world at that moment.

XIV.

General Wyngarde watched the horror unfolding in the hallowed halls of the Pentagon from the underground bunker he and all the other top brass had been ferried to during the lockdown. He wasn't happy being down there when civvies were being slaughtered wholesale by those...those *things*.

He walked up to the needle-dick kid posted at the door to the bunker. Didn't even look old enough to buy his own beer. *It takes all kinds*, the man thought to himself.

"Step aside, Junior," Wyngarde growled. "And hand over that peashooter of yours."

The boy, face covered with an unfortunate case of adult acne, sputtered and clutched his AK-47 to his chest like a security blanket.

Senator Laura Powers walked up to the two men. "Albert, what do you think you're doing?"

The General narrowed his eyes at the soldier for another moment before turning his attention to the senator. He knew her through her third ex-husband, an old buddy of his. The woman was a battle axe and while he wouldn't consider her a friend, he certainly respected the hell out of her. "You and I both know I should be up there fighting those hellspawned creatures, Powers. Not hiding down here with you and all these...these... pencil-necks!"

If any of said pencil-necks took umbrage with his statement, they wisely stayed quiet.

"Going up there is suicide, Albert." The woman placed her hand on his arm, a pacifying gesture he was all too familiar with. Ruby used to use the same technique whenever the Ravens were losing.

Wyngarde gritted his teeth. "And how am I supposed to live with myself if I stay down here shaking in my booties while innocent men and women die upstairs?"

The Senator and the General went back years. He knew full well that she knew better than to argue with him when he put his mind to something. The woman turned to the sweating boy in uniform.

"Son, go on and give the General your rifle."

"B-but, Senator-"

She *tut-tutted* the boy and he obeyed, handing Wyngarde the assault rifle. The General slung it around his shoulder.

"Now, open that damn door and let me do my job for Pete's sake."

The kid did so without a fuss.

"Albert?"

Wyngarde looked over his shoulder at the Senator. "Yeah, Senator?"

"Be careful."

"I'd tell you Careful was my middle name but we both know it's Yancy."

He saw a hint of a smile on the Senator's face as he left the safety of the bunker and made his way topside to join the fight. *I still got it*, the General thought to himself, a smile on his own threatening to emerge from the corners of his chapped lips.

Standing before the steel partition that sealed the bunker off from the rest of the Pentagon, Wyngarde entered the access code. The partition raised, he ducked under it, and it lowered again. Three of the demons or zombies or whatever the hell they were supposed to be were feasting on some poor, dead son of a bitch. Sensing his presence, all three turned to look at him, rising simultaneously. The one closest to him had a bloody grin plastered on its leathery face.

As he stared down the corpse-women, a snippet of *Revelation: 6* came to mind. Or maybe it was the Johnny Cash interpretation. Considering that Wyngarde hadn't set foot into a church since they'd baptized Martin, it was very likely the latter.

And I heard a voice in the midst of the four beasts,
And I looked and behold a pale horse:
And his name, that sat on him, was Death.
And Hell followed with him.

"Alright, ladies," he said, the whisper of a smile turning to a full-blown grin as he clicked the rifle's safety off, "*come get some.*"

And Hell followed with him.

XV.

The giant metal gate separated Marjorie from the interior of the pentagonal building. There was some sort of puzzle to opening it that involved entering a numerical code in a certain order. She was already frantic and being stuck outside as the Valkyrie were terrorizing the innocent people of this world was not making matters any better.

She wished she could ask d'Argetan what to do.

Grinding her teeth, she tried another code. The gate made an angry noise at her and a small, red, inset crystal on the number pad blinked brightly.

"Damn it," Marjorie grunted.

Sensing a presence, she spun around to see a corpse-woman staring at her, its skeletal held tilted. It had a large, curved blade in its hand.

"I don't have time for you right now," she told the dread thing as she made two quick slashes that left the creature in three pieces on the ground, its weapon beyond its reach. Marjorie turned back to the puzzle in front of her.

A thought occurred: magic wasn't completely gone from this world. She still had *some* connection to her abilities. Mayhap a lightning bolt applied to the numbered pad would open the gate. It was worth a try.

Placing her right hand open-palmed against the pad, Marjorie released a jolt of electricity. The pad made a happier noise and the gate raised, granting her access. A small victory, but a victory all the same.

"Finally," she whispered, allowing herself a brief sigh of relief.

The hallway that stood before her gave the monster hunter pause. Some sort of light flashed red at a steady pace and a voice informed the empty hallway that the building, the 'Pentagon' apparently, was under 'lockdown.' Those words were unfamiliar, but Marjorie used context to figure it out. Somebody had activated a sort of defensive spell or mechanism upon the arrival of the Valkyrie which resulted in the gates lowering and cutting off access. It was smart.

Steeling herself, Marjorie entered the building to look for survivors.

XVI.

"Damn it!" Jack grunted as the keypad beeped angrily at him again.

Jefferson sighed. It was Jack's tenth or eleventh attempt at using ancient key codes to open the partition. He hoped June was okay, wherever she was. The zombies couldn't have gotten that far into the Pentagon before the lockdown had been activated. Hopefully she was safe and sound in the break room.

"We're trapped," Cara muttered. She was sitting on the ground, staring vacantly at a square of tile.

"No," Jack said. "I refuse that." He tried another code. Another angry beep. Another curse. Rinse, lather, repeat.

Then, from the other side of the partition, gunfire could be heard. All heads snapped to attention, staring at the blockade.

It opened. Cara squeaked with surprise or maybe fear. Jefferson didn't know which.

The figure on the other side gripped an AK-47. The man was easily in his mid-sixties with a bald head and the faintest whisper of a gray goatee. From his attire, Jefferson could tell he was a general with the U.S. Army. A quick glance to his left confirmed it, as Jack was saluting.

"At ease, soldier," the man said, his voice raspy with age. "Give me a sit-rep."

"We've got civilians with us, we're cut off from the rest of the building," Jack told the man. "My partner here has been separated from his daughter and there are an unknown number of hostiles that have infiltrated the building from points unknown. They appear to be nearly unkillable, but I've found that a little de-limbing goes a long way." He stopped, then his eyes widened and he added, "Sir."

The general nodded. "The situation ain't FUBAR just yet. How many of you have fired a gun before?"

Jack, Jefferson, and Tom all raised their hands.

"Alright, here's what we're gonna do," the general said, looking at Jack. "We're gonna get this little lady here somewhere safe, then we're gonna load up at the armory, find your man's daughter, then send these zombie bastards back to Hell. Name's Wyngarde."

The men introduced themselves. Cara didn't say anything, just stared wide-eyed at the general.

"You alright, miss?" Wyngarde asked her.

The woman replied with a sad, shell-shocked shrug. Wyngarde looked at Tom. "Help her up, son. Let's find us a base of operations to put her down in."

"Sir," Tom replied, helping Cara to her feet. She seemed not to want to stand on her own volition, so he lifted her up and carried her in his arms.

"These things are savage, but they don't seem to move very fast," Wyngarde explained. "Stick behind me, stay close, stay alert. Let's move out."

Wyngarde led them in the general direction of the Legal department's offices. Jefferson knew it was in the opposite direction from the break room but at the same time, it was only two doors down from the armory. He wasn't a religious man by any stretch but all the same, he found himself thanking whatever god might be listening for delivering unto them such a badass old warhorse.

XVII.

The Coffer Corpse starred at them, not moving. Roger felt liquid warmth along his leg as his bladder released its contents. He ignored the embarrassing but not entirely unpleasant sensation and tried to think of something, anything, to do to stop whatever horrible thing was about to happen.

Looking around him, his eyes fell on a fire ax under glass. Thinking only of the woman and little girl with him, he balled his meaty hand into a fist and punched the glass. It shattered and he removed the red, metal ax from its home and turned to the Coffer Corpse.

"Roger, don't," Alex whispered.

Roger had never made a difference. He had never mattered. If he was the subject of his own *It's a Wonderful Life*, his guardian angel would've been dreadfully disappointed to discover how little his not existing would've impacted the lives of those around him.

But this was his chance to make a difference. His chance to matter. He could save these people and be a hero.

With that thought in his mind the man ran, truly ran, for the first time in his adult life. The ax over his head, he let out the scream of a warrior. With as much force as he could muster, Roger drove the ax square into the monster's skull. It went several inches in and stuck there.

Roger stared at the corpse-woman, unsure of whether or not it had been felled by his might.

As it drove its gnarled hand through his chest, it became abundantly clear that his efforts mattered naught. He had failed.

72

Roger's mother had always told him he'd had a big heart, but seeing it in the thing's hand was the first time that he'd ever had actual proof. As the man fell to his knees, his lifeblood leaking out at an alarming rate, he wanted to apologize to June and Alex for failing them, for failing his niece, for failing himself.

Instead, he just died as he had lived: fat, useless, and full of regret.

XVIII.

The fists banging on the door seemed relentless. Nigel ignored them, watching the monitors. General Wyngarde had met up with the two guys from the Social Media department, some girl with a sword had made her way into the building, and people were dying all over the place.

His eyes flicking from screen to screen, Nigel found himself hypnotized by the events playing out before him. Revulsion had given way to an interest beyond morbid. All the extreme horror and splatterpunk books he'd read by guys like Jack Ketchum and Edward Lee had nothing on the Mutilated Viking Stripper Massacre.

Suddenly, Nigel had a moment of clarity. He pulled out a notepad and scribbled something down: "Mutilated Viking Stripper Massacre – title of book if I survive this."

Taking a handful of Sun Chips and absentmindedly shoving them into his mouth, the man returned his attention to the monitors. The banging on the door from outside continued but he paid it no mind.

The HR chick with the nice tits and the little girl were about to get it.

XIX.

June screamed again. Alex was too scared to scream, herself. She just gaped at Roger's body and the undead monster that had torn his heart from his chest.

"S-stay behind me, June," she said, her voice cracking. The girl didn't respond, but she had stopped screaming.

The rotting corpse reached up and pulled at the fire ax that was lodged in its skull. After several moments, it came free. It looked at the ax and grinned then turned its attention to Alex and June.

They were screwed. All Alex had on her was a can of mace and what was *that* going to do to a zombie? Not only were they helpless against the undead thing in the steel bikini, but now it had a fire ax to butcher them with.

Without warning, the monster fell to pieces. Behind it stood a beautiful red-headed woman that was dressed like somebody cosplaying their OC from a *Vampire Hunter D* fanfic. The woman picked up the ax, flipped it around and extended it handle-first to Alex.

"My name is Marjorie Isabella Lenoir of the Lenoir Monster Hunters. Who might you be?"

Alex took the ax and just stared at the woman. She was beautiful, ethereal even. Pale skin, hair like fire, and an air of confidence about her that Alex wished she possessed within herself. "I'm, uh, Alexandra Dubois of the Department of Defense Human Resources Department."

Marjorie smiled at her then turned to June. "And who are you, little one?"

"*June*," the girl whispered.

75

"We're trying to get her back to her dad. Can you help us?"

The woman nodded. "Of course, but we must be quick. I need to find whatever it is the Valkyrie are looking for and destroy it before they can bring it back to the Lich."

"Valkyrie? The Lich?" Alex asked, feeling very lost.

Marjorie gestured to the corpse on the ground, slowly dragging its upper half by the one remaining arm in their direction. "The Lich is the most powerful necromancer in the realm of Arcania and that," she paused, severing the thing's arm, "is a Valkyrie, one of the animated corpses under his control. He is controlling them from the other side of the portal and all I know for sure is that they are looking for something that is hidden somewhere in your Pentagon."

"Sure, okay," Alex said. Who was she to argue after watching the skeletal remains of a woman in a Thor helmet tear the heart from a man's chest?

"Now, which way is the girl's father?" Marjorie asked.

June turned and pointed to the opposite end of the hallway from where Marjorie had appeared. "He's that way, but the door came down and we can't get through," she whimpered.

"Leave that to me," the redhead woman said, approaching the partition.

"Do you know the code?" Alex asked, immediately feeling silly when she realized that there was no way someone from another world would have any idea what the passcode would be.

Alex watched, cheeks burning, as Marjorie placed her hand against the keypad and emitted some sort of electrical shock to it, causing the partition to raise. She turned to her and smiled. "No, but I know how to cheat."

She had a feeling that Marjorie probably didn't know what an emoji was, but if she did, the monster hunter might recognize the look on the other woman's face as the emoji with hearts for eyes.
"Come now, quickly," the monster hunter urged, setting off down the hall.

Taking June by the hand, Alex followed.

Act Three:
Hooah

I.

Senator Laura Powers took a sip from her flask and grimaced as the warm liquor trickled down her throat. She typically didn't drink vodka straight, not since college, but there weren't any good mixers in the bunker underneath the Pentagon. If they made it out alive, she would have to do something about that.

People were dying. Good, innocent people. And while they died, Senator Powers got to kick up her heels in a temperature-controlled bunker with a handful of other people deemed important enough to keep alive in case of emergency, the emergency in this case apparently being an incursion by extra-dimensional zombie women. She looked over at the two pimple-faced soldiers who didn't look like they'd ever pulled the trigger of their guns much less kissed a girl and took another sip from her flask..

The Senator's eyes fell on the bust of John F. Kennedy in the corner. She'd met him once, back in '62. She was still in law school, had been invited to a function by some flash-in-the-pan senator barely older than the children guarding her in the bunker. She wasn't impressed. But the bust in the corner, regardless of what President it represented, it was important.

And what lay behind it was far, far more important.

Powers took another swig from her flask and waited.

II.

The feeling walking into the armory inspired within Jack was akin to a kid walking into a candy shop with a crisp ten dollar bill clutched in their grubby little hand. The armory was not accessible by anyone that didn't have at least a Triple Eagle clearance level and ever since he had been dumped in the Social Media department, Jack was stuck with clearance level 'Eaglet.'

The room was at least three times the size of the Social Media department, filled wall-to-wall with all kinds of weaponry, with several racks in the middle of the room similarly filled with even more guns.

"This is awesome," he whispered out loud as he lifted up a jet-black semi-automatic combat shotgun. It was like something out of that *Call to Arms: Fight for the Future* game he'd seen commercials for.

"She's a beaut, isn't she?" The General asked him.

"She sure is, sir," Jack marveled.

"The Roosevelt Global Penetrator Semi-Automatic Shotgun: for when you absolutely, positively have to vaporize undead bitches from hell," Wyngarde said with a small smile.

At the mention of Roosevelt Global, Jack's eyes glazed over. Suddenly he was back home. There was just a hint of sun on the horizon. Jack was coming home after a long night of staking out Roosevelt Global. He'd received a tip that one of the company's off-the-books scientists was working on a secret project at their Maryland branch's lab, some sort of super-flu that would turn people into psychotic animals, but there had been no sign of the guy.

He slipped off his shoes and hung up his coat, then snuck upstairs as quietly as possible lest he disturb Bethany or the girls. It was winter break, so Jenny and Georgia got to sleep in.

Wincing as the door to his bedroom creaked as he opened it, Jack froze. Bethany didn't stir and he let out a sigh of relief. The woman had the patience of a saint when it came to his working all sorts of crazy hours, but waking her up was like waking up a dragon: an all-around terrible idea.

He had stripped down to his skivvies and slid under the sheets before he noticed something was wrong. The bed was wet, sticky. Goosebumps erupted across his body as Jack's stomach started doing gymnastics.

Bethany was a notoriously light sleeper but she didn't respond when he tried to shake her awake.

"No," he muttered, "no, no, no." He got out of bed and turned on the light.

Their white sheets had been turned burgundy with blood. Jack looked down at his bare legs and saw them stained with that same awful color. Far away, he heard himself continuing to chant "no" like a mantra, as if he were to say it enough times it would undo what had been done.

Bethany had been covered with the sheet, a blessing in disguise. But why was there so much blood? What had they done to her?

Then, he thought of the girls.

Running to their room, not even feeling the pain of hitting the stupid nick-knack cabinet Bethany insisted they keep in the upstairs hallway (the doctor would tell him later that morning that he'd broken his pinkie toe), Jack flicked on their light.

Just like their mother, the girls were in their beds covered entirely with their blood-stained sheets.

Falling to his knees, the mantra of no's become much louder and longer, filled with the pain and agony of a man whose entire world had just been shattered. Some neighbor, he didn't know who, called the cops.

Life had become something of a blur after that.

"Jack, you still with us?" The voice that shook him from his trance belonged to Jefferson.

Jack blinked a few times and looked at him. The kid was strapped, having swapped the hammer for twin Uzis and his own Penetrator slung across his back. "Yeah, I'm fine. Sorry."

Jack looked at the other two men. Tom had a slick chrome automatic rifle with a grenade launcher and a nasty-looking bayonet attached while the General had two Desert Eagles and a machete on his back.

"You sure, son? I don't need you losing it out there in the shit," Wyngarde said, his eyes piercing Jack.

Jack cocked his Penetrator. "I'm sure, sir."

A hint of a smile flashed across the General's face. "Good. Now let's go find Mr. Brody's daughter."

III.

The Lich grew impatient. He knew that controlling the Valkyrie across dimensions would have certain complications, but he had underestimated the effectiveness of the Lenoir girl and the handful of humans that had taken up arms against the Valkyrie. The fact that someone had activated a defense mechanism in the structure was also affecting the progress in retrieving the relic.

He decided to split the focus of the Valkyrie threefold. One third of the remaining Valkyrie would continue to pursue the relic, another third would find out how to deactivate the pentagonal structure's defenses, and the final third would track down little Marjorie Lenoir and her new friends and tear them apart piece by bloody piece.

The Lich had spent long enough divining the location of the Wellspring. It would be his, even if that meant crossing over and getting it himself.

A skeleton in a bow tie entered his chambers and presented him with a goblet of virgin's blood. He took it and waved the skeleton away. As he drank deeply, the Lich thought that when controlling such a large army of corpses, it was important to stay hydrated.

IV.

Most of the monitors had grown boring. After the wholesale slaughter had ended, Nigel found that there were really only two subplots left that he felt invested in: the General and his team of makeshift warriors in one corner and the redhead with the sword, the busty HR chick, and the little girl on the other. All the other monitors were largely static images of corpses, interrupted only by the occasional Mutilated Viking Stripper (ever since coming up with the title of his book, he thought of them in proper punctuation) passing by.

The lull in the action reminded him of his only real issue with Stephen King's *The Stand*. Once the 99.9% of the population had died of Captain Tripps and the survivors had gravitated to Mother Abigail or Randall Flagg, things kind of slowed down. In fact, his favorite part of King's *Cell* was when shit had first hit the fan and everybody was killing each other wholesale in city streets.

Nigel reached into the bag of Sun Chips for another handful only to discover there were only crumbs left. That left him with a Cliff bar and half of a room temperature Mountain Dew. As he watched the female half of the story make their way through the desolate hallways of the Pentagon, he found himself hoping that something exciting would happen soon.

Thinking about *The Mutilated Viking Stripper Massacre*, Nigel made the conscious decision that there wouldn't be any boring fluff between the slaughter and the climax. Just balls-to-the-wall blood, guts, and bullets, the way it should be.

The banging on the door to the nerve center of the Pentagon had increased dramatically, but the man was far too engrossed in the source material of his future Bram Stoker award-winning novel to notice.

V.

June was scared. It wasn't so much that there were zombie women running around killing people like Roger, who was really super nice; it was that she knew the adults were scared too. Alex couldn't stop whimpering and the lady with the red hair wouldn't take her hand off of the grip of her sword. The fact that she was gripping it so hard it made her knuckles go white hadn't escaped the eleven-year-old.

She'd never seen her dad get scared. He was always happy and smiling and telling jokes. It made her sad sometimes, only because she knew nobody could be happy all the time and knew that at least some of the time, even if she wasn't around, her dad would have to let the sad in.

Just because she was a kid didn't mean she was stupid. She knew it was her mom that messed up their family, but she also knew that her dad took the blame because he knew what it would do to her mother if June knew that it was her fault.

One day, several years after what one man had dubbed *The Mutilated Viking Stripper Massacre*, June would learn the definition of martyr and immediately think of her father. She knew that she was his whole world and could only guess that getting to see her every other weekend must've been like having to eat Brussels sprouts times a thousand. Her prepubescent mind was only months away from fully grasping the fact that his sacrifice was the reason why he drank on the weeknights like that awful Heather girl from Mrs. Hoffman's class's dad and why he took home so many ladies he didn't really care about. There was a hole in his heart.

That was what made June saddest.

But it was that childish semi-understanding of what he had done that kept her from hating her mother. She knew that if she did give in, did tell her mom what a terrible person she was for splitting up their perfect little family, that all he had given up would have been for nothing.

Lost in thought, June bumped into Alex. Snapping out of her daze, the girl saw that they had come to another one of the metal gates. The other lady, Marjorie, looked at them.

"Ready?"

June nodded. The woman placed a hand against the keypad thing and then shocked it like Conductor from the old *The Spartans* comics her dad let her read. The gate lifted. June braced herself in case one of the monster ladies was waiting for them.

There was nothing on the other side.

June followed closely as Marjorie led them down the hall. Suddenly, Marjorie stopped, holding up a hand that June had come to know meant "Hold up." The woman gestured to a closed door. There was a piece of paper taped to it that read: "SAFE ROOM. KNOCK THREE TIMES, PAUSE, KNOCK AGAIN."

June watched as Marjorie looked from left to right, then knocked three times, paused, and knocked a fourth time.

The sound of something heavy being moved out of the way could be heard from the other side of the door and then it opened. An Asian lady with runny make-up stood there. Her face lit up when she saw Alex.

"*You're alive!*" she whispered, throwing her arms around the other woman. Then, the new lady looked down at June. "*Are you June?*" she asked.

June nodded.

"I'm Cara. Your daddy helped save me. He's looking for you right now."

The news that her father was okay filled June with hope. She turned to Marjorie, who squatted down, bringing her to June's level.

"Will you find my dad?"

Marjorie smiled and nodded. *"You stay with Alex, I'll find your dad."*

June smiled for the first time since the alarm started going off. *"Thank you."* She threw her arms around Marjorie in a big hug, which the woman returned in kind.

"Be careful," Alex told Marjorie as the redhead stood upright.

June saw the way that Alex looked Marjorie and it reminded her exactly of how her dad used to look at her mom. Hannah Lang had two moms and Gregory Sanderson had two dads, and June's father had taught her long ago that there was nothing wrong with something like that.

Marjorie reached out and placed a hand on Alex's shoulder. June watched as the two women locked eyes. Marjorie smiled and nodded and then, she was on her way. As Cara shut the door and slid the desk back in front of it, June looked at Alex, who couldn't stop smiling. It made June happy for a fleeting second before she remembered that there were zombie ladies, 'Valkyrie' as Marjorie called them, all over the place trying to kill them all.

Sitting down in a nearby wheelie-chair, the girl sighed. She wanted her dad.

VI.

Tom felt just a tad out of his element. He worked in the Finance department, crunching numbers and slashing budgets, not fighting undead women from another dimension. When General Wyngarde asked who had shot a gun before, he hadn't been lying. It had just been a really long time.

Tom and his dad, Big Tom, used to go out at the crack of dawn on the first day of hunting season into the deep woods of Pennsylvania to go hunting for bucks. Tom hated it, but loved his dad, so he grinned and bore it for ten years. Then the cancer took Big Tom and just days before hunting season was set to kick off. Despite a decade of pretending he loved being up a tree on a rickety hunting platform in early December before the sun was even thinking about rising, Tom (now a young man) found himself alone in the middle of the woods, drinking beer and waiting for that twelve-point buck to enter his crosshairs.

But that was a decade ago and he hadn't touched a firearm since. Not until hell had broken loose at the Pentagon.

He had chosen the rifle almost entirely based on his knowledge of games like the *Call to Arms* series. While he wasn't much for hunting, stepping into the boots of a soldier in the near-future fighting against impossible odds against the invading armies of fictional countries led by despots played by famous actors was one of Tom's favorite pastimes. The rifle he'd chosen had a noob tube *and* a bayonet attached to it, which usually didn't happen until you at least hit level 27 (presuming you didn't preorder the game).

Of course, as he stepped over the lower half of one of his co-workers, Tom reminded himself that he wasn't playing a game at home on his couch in his underwear. It was very real and the enemy was very deadly.

"Not for nothing," he said, breaking the silence, "but at least we don't have to worry about the black guy dying first, am I right?"

The only reply came from the General, who grunted indifferently. Tom frowned. His attempt at levity had fallen flat, further reinforcing that he was indeed trapped in a hellish reality where monsters really did exist.

The quartet turned a corner and Tom saw one of the zombies at the far end of the hall. He raised his rifle, pressed the stock against his shoulder, took aim, and pulled the trigger.

The wrong trigger.

He launched a grenade at the wretched, skeletal thing. It exploded on contact, annihilating not only the zombie but also the wall next to it.

The wall that led to the central courtyard.

The very same central courtyard that was full of more zombie Viking women.

"Way to go, kid," the General muttered. "Out of the frying pan and into the motherfucking inferno." The General looked at Tom, Jefferson, and Jack. "Now might be a good time to make peace with whatever gods you answer to, boys." Then, to Tom's great surprise, Wyngarde grinned. "Let's give'm hell."

VII.

The story was finally picking back up!

An explosion! Just what the third act needed.

Nigel grinned, his eyes wide with excitement, as he watched the men enter Ground Zero and take the fight to the Mutilated Viking Strippers.

If he had to guess, the MVS's would manage to kill the black guy and maybe the General before they managed to take down the last of them, and then whatever opened the portal in the first place would emerge for a final battle, just in time for the warrior woman to meet up with them and send it back to Hell.

The stage was set. It was time for the climax. Everything was coming together!

Behind him, the door to the Pentagon's central nervous system finally gave and a swarm of Mutilated Viking Strippers poured in. Nigel paid them no mind as he watched the action unfold on the monitors.

One of what Nigel had come to think of as *his* titular monsters grabbed the man by his neck and lifted him out of his chair, then turned him to face it. At some point during the fracas, Nigel had gone quite insane and rather than fear for his life, he simply observed the wretched, shambling corpses that had entered his sanctuary.

The one that had him in its clutches spoke, its voice the squeaking of rusty bed springs from his mother's room as she entertained another Uncle John. "Lower the defenses," it growled.

Now *that* was an interesting wrinkle. Could it be that they had not yet come to the climax as he had previously thought? Was there still more story to be told?

90

"Sure thing," he said, a lunatic's smile plastered to his face.

The Mutilated Viking Stripper released him and Nigel turned back to the monitors. For a moment, his eyes lingered on the battle taking place at Ground Zero but he knew he had a job to do and he did it. A few keystrokes on his terminal and the lockdown was deactivated.

"There." He turned back to the Mutilated Viking Stripper. "So, what's next?"

His answer came in the form of skeletal thumbs digging into his eye sockets. All the Brian Keene books he'd read in his lifetime and Nigel still didn't manage to see that coming.

As the creatures he'd cast as the antagonists in a story he'd very clearly never have the opportunity to write tore him open, Nigel thought to himself that *The Mutilated Viking Stripper Massacre* was a shitty title. *Mutilated Viking Strippers Take the Pentagon* was far superior.

With a mind that had long since crossed into uncharted territory, eyes that no longer saw and organs that no longer resided inside his body where they belonged, Nigel Daniels the would-be splatterpunk author died smiling.

VIII.

With the keep's defenses lowered, the Lich's Valkyrie could search for the Wellspring unimpeded. With a smile, the undead necromancer supped from his goblet. The virgin's blood was an excellent vintage, aged sixteen years.

With most of the human opposition occupied in the central area of the keep, plenty of his horde left, and the Lenoir girl on her own, it was only a matter of time before they fell before the sheer numbers of his forces. Then the Wellspring would be in his hands and Ultimate Power would be his. Woe unto those who would stand against him.

Deciding to indulge himself, the Lich let out a maniacal laugh. He couldn't help it.

"Is everything alright, sir?" one of his skeleton servants asked him.

The Lich turned around and glared at his intrusive minion. "What have I told you cretins about interrupting me while I'm maniacally laughing?"

The skeleton shrugged. "You have a lot of rules. It's really hard to keep track of them all."

With a flick of his wrist, the skeleton was incinerated by a pale, green eldritch flame.

Good help was so hard to find when it came to the undead.

IX.

The explosion stole Marjorie's attention almost instantly. It had been close by. Whether or not it was June's father and the men he was with, there were likely survivors that she could help.

She made her way in the direction the explosion came from.

As she made her way, the keep's defenses were lowered. Marjorie knew that was a bad sign as the Valkyrie hadn't gone anywhere. She suspected the Lich had somehow found a way to deactivate the defenses and now the Valkyrie would have nearly unrestricted access to all five wings of the pentagonal stronghold.

What was he looking for? If she knew that, she would at least have something to go on. As it was, all she could do was dismember the Valkyrie and save as many people as she could.

Finally, she found the hallway the explosion had come from. A gaping hole in the wall led out to the central courtyard where she saw four men fighting for their lives against the Valkyrie.

Gripping Finem, Marjorie ran to join them.

X.

When the lockdown ended and the lights came back on, Cara nearly jumped out of her skin.

"What? What is it?" Alex asked her. The, she looked around and realized what had happened. "Is it over?"

Cara shook her head. "I don't...it can't be, can it? Marjorie only just left." She was terrified, and with good reason, but then again Cara had always been fearful. It was something she was working on with her therapist.

It started when she was fifteen and working off the books in her father's little shop in downtown DC. They had been robbed and her father had been shot. He survived but had a permanent limp. Cara was physically fine but the encounter had left her afraid of her own shadow. That was why she went into accounting: the risk was minimal and somebody always needed their books balanced.

Her friend Jenna worked at the Pentagon and when the position in their Finance department opened up, Cara had jumped at the opportunity. Working in the Department of Defense? What could be safer than that?

If her face wasn't locked in a toothy grimace of fear, Cara would've scowled at the irony of her current situation.

"The door is locked, right?" she asked Alex.

Alex nodded. "Yes."

Cara gripped the pistol that the General had left her with. The walking corpses, 'Valkyrie' according to Marjorie, were practically unkillable, but they could be hobbled. Cara had spent a good amount of time at the shooting range, a factoid she'd decided to leave out when Wyngarde has asked them who had experience shooting a gun lest she get dragged along to fight the Valkyrie. Instead, she was barricaded in the finance department with Alex and Jefferson Brody's daughter, a veritable buffet for animated (not *re*animated as Alex had pointed out while filling Cara in after the monster hunter left) corpse women just waiting to happen.

A thought occurred to her just then: if the lockdown was over that meant that they could escape.

"Alex," she said, her voice flat.

"Yeah?"

She looked at Alex, well aware of the wide-eyed, crazy look on her own face. "We can get out of here. Out of the Pentagon."

Alex shook her head. "No Cara, we should stay here until Marjorie comes back. We don't know what's out there!"

"If we stay here, what's to stop one of the Valkyrie from hacking down the door with an ax? At least out there we stand a chance of escaping!" She ran over to the desk and began shoving it out of the way.

"Cara, no!"

Cara turned the pistol on Alex who flinched instinctively. "You can come with me and make a run for it or stay and wait for death. No offense, but I don't really care which one you choose."

The terrified woman finished moving the desk barricade and unlocked the door. She cast one last glance over her shoulder at Alex and the little girl before she opened the door. "See ya."

Then fearful little Cara Hahn set off into the unknown, feeling almost brave for the first time in her life.

Act Four:
The Department of Immigration Studies

It sounded like a warzone upstairs. Senator Powers, her head swimming as the vodka had gone above and beyond its call of duty, sat in a cushy chair and lamented the fact that her flask was empty. Of all of the top personnel that had absconded to the secret bunker beneath the Pentagon, she was the only one that had any idea as to what the animated corpses were, where they had come from and what it was that they wanted.

Laura Powers, the wealthy, thrice-divorced, relatively mild mannered, 74-year-old conservative senator from Dallas Texas, had been part of a clandestine group of government officials that dealt with otherworldly happenings for over thirty years.

The first time something had crossed over was in 1982. Whatever it was, it hadn't survived the trip. She had been forty-one, and it was her first term as a senator. Her addition to the group, on the books as the Department of Immigration Studies (rather tongue-in-cheek, all things considered) was pure chance. She just happened to have been in the right place at the wrong time.

Laura and her second husband Wilbur, the one whose name she chose to keep as Powers had a great ring to it, were in DC for some charity event. The event was the next day and Wilbur had left the hotel for one of those discrete little Washington, DC hotels to fuck his little ginger mistress with the usual excuse of "grabbing drinks with Mitch and Lou."

Mitch and Lou, ostensibly war buddies from Korea, didn't exist, at least not as far as physical proximity to any bar or watering hole in the District of Columbia. Laura knew this, *had* known this, but she was biding her time and waiting for the right moment to drop the bomb. It was like a game for her and it was a game that she played very well. As her youngest daughter Annie, still four years away from being born in '82, would say, Laura was a 'bad bitch,' plain and simple. It was that defining characteristic that had served her so well in the game of politics and almost as well in her personal life.

While Wilbur spent his oil baron money sweating all over a nineteen-year-old redheaded liberal arts major, Laura had gone for a walk down to the Lincoln Memorial Reflecting Pool. It had always been her favorite place in the Mall. She stood on the far side from the Washington Monument (a phallic tribute if there ever was one) and watched the late summer wind send ripples across the water.

It was late July, the humidity was truly disgusting, and as far as Laura could tell, it was just her and two men whom she would later come to know very well sitting on the steps to the Lincoln Memorial.

It was 10:43 PM Eastern Standard Time when the thing came through, a time she remembered as her watch had stopped. There was a noise like a choir of nail guns going off all at once was heard and the thing fell from a hole in the sky some thirty feet above the Reflecting Pool and splashed down with a meaty thud.

Just looking at the thing made Laura feel like she was going to lose her mind. It was all eyes and tentacles and hair and she hated it, *hated it* and she just wanted to go and wait at the hotel and take the bible in the nightstand and make that cheating son of a bitch eat page after page until his stomach burst and then the two men that had been sitting on the steps of the Lincoln Memorial leapt into action. They pulled out some sort of retro-futuristic ray guns straight out of a 50's sci-fi movie and vaporized the thing with beams of orange energy. It was like it had never been there at all.

Laura screamed and screamed until one of the men, a black man with a military crew cut, grabbed her and shook her. "It's okay! It's okay!" he told her.

The other man, a waifish little goblin of a man with long, greasy blond hair sneered. "Just give'r a slap, Tom. She's clearly hysterical."

"Stow it, Gordon," the man with the crew cut growled. He turned back to Laura. "Mrs. Powers, it's going to be okay."

Hearing her name brought Laura back to reality. "How do you know my name?"

The man released her. "I watch a lot of C-Span, ma'am. The name's Thomas Ulysses, United States Marine Corps. The social reject in desperate need of a haircut is Wiley Gordon. He's what you might call an independent contractor."

"Hey," the greasy-haired man said. Laura noticed his the lenses of his glasses were thicker than Wilbur's billfold.

She struggled to find her words, a sensation she was not used to in the slightest. After her mouth opened and shut several times, she finally came out with, "What the hell was that thing? Who are you people?"

"I'm afraid that's classified, Senator," Ulysses told her.

"Fuck that, Tom. You ever read H.P. Lovecraft, lady?" Gordon asked her.

"Wiley-" Ulysses began before Laura cut him off.

"I'm not much for fiction."

The man rolled his eyes. "Well, that thing we just vaporized was what I've classified as a Minor Horror. They're able to get through every once in a blue moon where the walls of reality have become too thin. Fortunately these holes are too small for anything more than a Minor Horror to come through." He paused, took his glasses off, wiped the lenses with his shirt. "Otherwise, we'd be fucked."

"Language, young man," Laura scolded.

Another eye-roll. Laura would put money on the fact that the too-thin man in a stained Frank Zappa T-shirt had little to no experience with talking to women and a problem with authority figures bigger than John Hinckley, Jr.'s erotomanic obsession with Jodie Foster.

"Anyway, once they come through, the barrier between our reality and theirs resets itself. The trick is disposing of them before they can do any damage."

"That's where these come in," Ulysses chimed in, holding up his ray gun. "Our friend here is, for better or for worse, something of a super-genius. He designed this guns as well as a method of divining where the walls of reality are weakest."

"They look like something out of some B-movie you'd see at the drive-in," Laura said, and they did. The ray guns were the size of a pistol, colored gold with a dark gray trigger, had three small gold dials on the left side, and were tipped with red, conical barrels.

Gordon smiled, revealing teeth in desperate need of a trip to the dentist. "That's by design. I'm a big sci-fi guy. I dig the general aesthetic of the whole cheesy 50's era of the genre."

Laura waved a dismissive hand and turned to Ulysses. "Mr. Ulysses, who are you people?"

Thomas Ulysses shrugged. "We don't have an official name yet. Gordon calls us Lovecraft's Angels."

"Quaint," Laura said, pursing her lips. "Is it just you two?"

"For now," Gordon said. "Tom here is the only one I trust not to bring this to The Man. I don't trust the government as far as I can throw them and I know that the stooges in the White House would ship these things off to Area 51 or some other place to cut them up and try to learn from them. The only thing we need to learn from these things is how to kill them quicker. You felt what it can do and the thing was already dead when it came through. Can you imagine one of them popping up in a place like Grand Central Station or out in Hollywood and we weren't there to stop them? It'd be a fucking massacre."

Senator Laura Powers chewed on her lower lip and nodded slightly. The thing got inside her head and made her think terrible things. She might loathe Wilbur and his inability to keep it in his pants but killing him was an utterly repellent thought.

She looked at the two men and said something that would change all of their lives forever: "Something has to be done about this. We'll need to get ourselves a new department to operate from as a cover. That way we can have a base of operations that isn't confined to our mothers' basements and a budget and people, good people, to help us keep the people of America safe."

"Whoa, whoa, whoa, lady. You can't just come in here and take over the operation."

"What do you do for a day job, Mr. Gordon?" Laura asked him.

The man narrowed his eyes. "Why?"

"Answer the question, Wiley," Thomas instructed, holding back a grin.

Gordon looked at his feet. "I...work at a video store."

"Well, how would you like to make $60,000 a year protecting your country from extra-dimensional tentacle monsters and the like instead?"

"Yeah, okay, you twisted my arm."

One month later, after Laura greased some wheels and called in a few favors, the three of them moved into the Department of Immigration Studies. It was a small, unassuming building several miles away from the Pentagon. The first and second floors were converted into offices while they moved all of Wiley's equipment into the basement. Neither man relished the thought of working a desk job by day, but it was necessary for them to make the Department of Immigration Studies an actual, functioning government building. They all brought people in that they thought they could trust and those people maintained budgets and developed programs and answered phones and read studies and nobody thought twice about the DIS.

That was exactly how they liked it.

With a budget that was approximately four times more than they actually needed to function on paper, Wiley was able to build bigger and better tools to monitor the places where reality was weakest across the entire globe. Fortunately for "Lovecraft's Angels," there were no more than three incidences a year.

It was one particular incident in 1994 that served as the catalyst for the horror show that was unfolding in the Pentagon.

April 5th, 1994 was a tragic day for many but nobody knew it yet. It wouldn't be until three days later that people would know that Kurt Cobain, the tortured singer of the band Nirvana, had killed himself when a man named Gary Smith came to install some security lighting.

But on the day that Cobain took a shotgun and made a liar out of himself where the lyrics of 'Come As You Are' were concerned, a man appeared out of nowhere in a field in Hillsville, Virginia. Captain Thomas Ulysses, field leader of "Lovecraft's Angels," and a squad of unassuming office workers who also doubled as highly-trained soldiers keeping the country safe from whatever creatures lay beyond their level of reality were there to greet him.

Two hours later, Senator Laura Powers found herself in the basement of the Department of Immigration Studies with Wiley Gordon (who over the two decades since they'd met had become far less insufferable and far more professional, to everyone's great delight), sitting across a handcuffed wizard.

"Actually," the handsome man with the dark brown goatee and piercing gold eyes corrected her, "I'm a *warlock*. Important difference. Wizards spend their lives with their noses buried in books, learning magic theory. Warlocks, on the other hand, are battle mages. We take what we've learned and we use it fight our enemies."

"Well," Wily began, "I guess that begs the question: Are you a good witch or a bad witch?"

The man smiled. "I assure you, I am on the side of the angels. As a matter of fact, it is why I've come to your world. I believe you have my Bag of Holding under lock and key."

"'Bag of Holding?' What is this, *Dungeons and Dragons*?" Wiley asked, a big, shit-eating grin on his face.

The warlock smiled and it made Laura feel something she hadn't felt in a long time. This man was, if nothing else, incredibly attractive. He had long silver hair and fair skin, piercing green eyes, and surprisingly soft features. "Pardon me if this is rude, but what would *you* know of dungeons *or* dragons, friend?"

104

Laura sighed. She had to stop the pissing match before it started. They didn't have time for it. "Wiley, be a dear and fetch our friend's Bag of Holding."

Begrudgingly, Wiley did as she asked. When he left the room, Laura looked at the man.

"Do you have a name, stranger?"

"Aye. And names have power. So until I'm sure we're on the same side I think mayhap I will keep it to myself."

"Fair. And where do you come from?"

"That, I will tell you. I come from the kingdom of Arcania, a place of magic and monsters. As of late, the dread necromancer known only as the Lich has begun amassing magical items to increase his power. That is why I have come here: to keep the most powerful source of magic in *any* realm out of his wretched hands."

Laura Powers had seen many things that defied explanation since that night in 1982, but the warlock was the first actual human being that they'd encountered from another world. The place he described sounded more like those *Castlevania* and *Zelda* games her son James was so fond of. But if things with hundreds of tentacles and the eyes to match could exist beyond the world they knew, why not a world of fantasy?

Wiley returned with the man's bag. He was pale.

"What's wrong, Wiley?" Laura asked him.

"It's real," he said, setting the bag down on the table. "I looked inside. It's...it's real. He's telling the truth."

105

The Senator glanced at the man. "Do I dare look inside?"

He grinned. "I wouldn't. It's like a sort of purple vortex. Hypnotizing, might make you sick. Now, would you like to remove my restraints or would you like to see me do it myself?"

She grinned. "I imagine I'd very much like to see the latter."

The last syllable was barely out of her mouth when the man was free from his cuffs. "Voilà!"

"Impressive," Laura told him. "Now, what's in this bag that's so important?"

The man picked up the bag. To the casual observer, it appeared to be a regular old burlap sack. But then, any illusion of normalcy was shattered as the Senator watched with amazement as he reached in with his arm and went far beyond what should've been physically possible. After rooting around inside his impossible bag, the warlock said, "Ah, here we are!"

He pulled out a small sphere that appeared to be made of some sort of glass. It glowed with a golden light and a thick white smoke swirled around inside. It was one of the most beautiful things Laura had ever seen and quite literally took her breath away.

"Now, here's some context for you: your realm is devoid of magic. Many realms, in my experience, start out the same way, with magic and science both existing hand in hand. As time goes on, many realms veer towards one or the other. I studied your realm at great length before coming here. Men used to cure blindness and disease with a touch, walk on water, and rise from the dead. And I mean, come on, do you really think the pyramids were the end result of some ancient marvel of engineering?"

Laura shrugged. "I mean, with enough slaves..."

The man smiled like one would when having a discussion about string theory with a toddler; kind but patronizing. "In any event, at some point science *won*. Magic disappeared. It happens. Now, more importantly, this bag in my hand contains a portal to a pocket dimension where I can keep the stuff that I find on my travels. It requires magic to function like so many items where I come from."

He paused, as if waiting for Laura or Wiley to catch on to something only he knew. When that didn't happen, he furrowed his brow momentarily and then continued.

"There is no magic in this realm. The bag should not function as anything more than a bag. I should be cut off from the Reaper's Scythe and the Armor of Sin and all the other things I've amassed and stored in that particular pocket dimension." He held up the sphere. "*But I'm not.* And it's because of this relic right here, the Wellspring. It is so immensely powerful on its own that it makes it possible for magic items to still function in a world where magic doesn't exist. Do you see now why I have brought it here?"

"You want to hide it here in our dimension and keep it away from the Lich," Laura said, finally understanding.

"Exactly. If the Lich were to gain possession of the Wellspring, he would become more powerful that any one being should ever be. He would be able to slay gods. The Wellspring must be kept from him at all costs."

Wiley stood up, perturbed. "If you were able to find our world, then what's to stop this Lich from coming through to take that thing himself? What if you bringing it here just paints a target on us?"

"Friend, I'm a mage. I know how to create protective wards. I can keep it safe from him finding it. We just need to dig a deep, deep hole to keep it hidden."

Laura Powers then made a decision that would come back to haunt her more than twenty years later. "I know just the place."

And so, with the mage's help, and some more greased palms and favors called in, a sub-basement that did not exist on any blueprint or document was built beneath the Pentagon. Laura's train of thought was a logical one (almost identical to that of the fearful Korean girl who was trying desperately to escape from a hell that the Senator herself was partly responsible for in the present): what location could be safer than the Pentagon? You needed both fingerprint scan and a retinal scan to access it and beyond that, the mage had placed over a dozen different wards on the room that would keep any scrying eyes from locating it.

Several months later, when they had completed their task, the mage emptied out his Bag of Holding and left all of the magical weapons, armor, and items he'd found on his travels and placed them around the room, turning it into an exhibit of sorts. Then, he looked at Laura.

"Senator, I appreciate everything you've done for me in my time here, but it is finally time for me to go."

"But where? You can't return home, the Lich would kill you! Why not come work for the Department of Immigration Studies? Help us defend our world."

The man shook his head. "Maybe one day I will return, but I must go out and see the wonders your world has to offer. I need to establish a new life. I need to find who I am in a world without magic."

Then the man took Laura's face in his hand and looked her in the eyes, which had filled with tears. "My name is Dran the Clever and it has been an honor to know you." And with that, he kissed her like she hadn't been kissed since she was a young woman. It was deep and full of passion, awakening fires in Laura that she'd forgot she'd had. But all too soon it was over and Dran the Clever was gone.

He never returned. No calls or letters. Laura didn't even know if he was still alive or even still in their world. It had made her bitter. That kiss had left an impression on her and she had waited for him for years before resigning herself to the fact that he probably found some vapid yoga instructor or Jamba Juice assistant manager to shack up with.

Returning to the present, the Senator didn't know what could've possibly happened to the wards Dran had placed that would've caused them to stop working, but they had and now the Lich had sent his minions through and they were killing people as they searched for the Wellspring.

Not only were the Lich's forces there because of a decision that she had made more than twenty years earlier, but there was no rescue coming either. Right after the lockdown had been triggered, as soon as the child soldier standing by the doorway to the bunker had come to take her to safety told her that zombies had appeared, the Senator had sent a message to the off-site location that dispatched the Pentagon Response Team telling them not to send anybody.

It had been protocol, reflex even. Any time something extra-dimensional happened, the DIS did whatever they could to keep things as contained as possible, but there had been no warning when the corpse-women came through, no time to think things through. The message couldn't be unsent and now Laura Powers and all the other poor bastards in the bunker were stuck between a rock and a hard place.

Even through her vodka-induced fog, she knew that before the day was over, there would be a reckoning.

109

Act Five:
Do Not Go Gentle

I.

Right before the redhead showed up, Jefferson was worried about his chances of survival. He'd expended both Uzis' magazines and it had barely made a dent in the horde. He had considerably better luck with the shotgun, but for every zombie he took down, two more took its place.

Everything was looking rather grim. The four men stood back-to-back, doing their best to thin the enemy's ranks but the fear of running out of ammo before the zombies ran out of limbs was very real.

"RELOADING!" the General cried out. He stood opposite Jefferson, so someone else would have to cover him. Jefferson took aim at the kneecap of a walking corpse with half its face missing and felt his stomach turn over when all he heard upon pulling the trigger was an impotent click.

He echoed the General's cry and hastily began trying to shove shells into the gun, but the high-stress situation the man found himself in didn't exactly lend itself to steady hands.

Just as the half-faced monster was on him, its body was split in half vertically. On the other side was a beautiful red-headed angel with a gore-streaked sword straight out of a video game. She simply gave him a nod and turned her attention to the next closest zombie.

What a woman, Jefferson thought as he made a second pass at reloading his shotgun.

II.

Cara could see the exit. It was just at the other end of the hall but to her it may as well have been miles. She hadn't seen any of the monster-women since she had left the others behind and that worried her. Maybe they all had gone to the central courtyard.

Maybe.

Constantly looking every which way, trying to reduce the likelihood of one of them getting the drop on her, Cara edged ever closer to freedom.

I'm really going to make it, she told herself. *I'm going to get out of here.*

Finally, after what felt like hours, she had reached the door. Just as she turned the handle, she felt a sharp pinch and her legs went out from under her. She fell to her side and could see her reflection in the glass of the door. There appeared to be a spear sticking out of her back. The fact that she could not feel her legs led Cara to deduce that the spear had severed her spinal column.

She was surprised to see her reflection smiling almost bashfully, as if it knew that counting her chickens before they hatched was the reason she was laying there on the ground, bleeding and paralyzed.

The fear was gone. There was no point in being scared anymore. Cara had spent her whole life being scared. God only knew how many things she'd missed out on in her life by living in fear. And now, the one-armed corpse was walking slowly toward her to finish her.

Last year at the Accounting Christmas party, the other people in her department had managed to drag her to the bar to celebrate with them. She had a virgin eggnog and watched her co-workers make asses of themselves. A handsome man who looked like he was an Abercrombie and Fitch model had approached her and tried talking to her. She could tell he was interested in, but the fears told her that it was all an act to lure her away from the flock so he could tear her apart. Rather than tell him she wasn't interested, Cara said she had to go to the bathroom and left the bar without even saying goodbye to her friends.

She knew that she could've had that man. She could have had a lot of men. Looking at herself in the reflection in the window, Cara knew that she was attractive. A little dowdy, sure, but not ugly by any stretch of the imagination. She could've been happy had she not let the fear rule her life.

The Valkyrie was getting closer. It had no eyes and its ribcage was wholly exposed.

She had never even been to prom. Her friend Mark had even asked her, but she told him her parents wouldn't let her go. The truth was she didn't even bother asking. Getting into a car accident with a drunk driver on the way home, getting date-raped, a gas main explosion; all those things seemed like inevitabilities. Cara felt silly as she thought of all the missed opportunities to have fun.

It was practically standing right on top of her.

While other girls were having sleepovers and giggling about boys and doing each other's make-up, thirteen-year-old Cara was watching her dad's *West Wing* box set, cuddled up underneath her comforter with a roll of cookie dough she'd snuck into her room.

Hers had been a lonely, solitary life and now, as the Valkyrie grabbed her by the hair and lifted her up off the ground, it was not fear that Cara felt. It was regret.

She simply looked into its eye sockets and waited.

It did not keep her waiting long.

III.

While most of the Lich's attention was focused on controlling the Valkyrie that were occupied in the keep's central courtyard, several of them continued to search for the Wellspring.

He could sense that it was close and put further focus into a Valkyrie that had just torn the throat out of a young woman who'd almost managed to escape. Controlling such a large horde proved to be nigh-impossible for even the most skilled necromancer, but the Lich was not just *any* necromancer.

Over a century earlier, he had just been a boy named Walton Stoneheart, son of Walter, living in a dreary little seaside hamlet in the northernmost part of Arcania known as Whitewharf. Walter was the town gravedigger and he and Walton eked out a miserable existence in a little shack in the graveyard on the hill that overlooked the town.

Walter was a bitter, cruel widower who loved to drink to excess almost as much as he loved to beat his son, whom he blamed for the death of Walton's mother during childbirth.

The children in the town wanted nothing to do with Walton just as their parents wanted nothing to do with his father, so Walton made the only friends he could: the corpses of the people his father dug graves for. He would talk to each of them long after they'd been buried for the simple fact that he had nobody else. They didn't talk back, but Walton didn't mind. They were great listeners.

One night in his twelfth year, long after his father had passed out in his own mess for the evening, Walton sat against the grave of a man named Jeremiah Mason and was in the middle of telling the dead man about how he was going to leave Whitewharf behind one day and make something of himself when he felt an odd tickle on the back of his neck, as if someone was watching him.

Walton stood up and saw an impeccably dressed man, complete with top hot and monocle, standing several graves over, looking at him. The man was tall and thin, *too* tall and thin, and his smile was far too large. And yet, Walton found himself rooted in place, unable to turn and run or even break the man's gaze.

"Hello, Walton," the man said. His voice was oddly soothing and sounded much closer to Walton than it should have.

"H-how do you know my name?" Walton asked.

"I know a great deal about you, Walton Stoneheart. Monsieur Gorden Nightshade III at your service." Then, the too-tall man bowed. The bow had a theatrical quality to it, like the circus performers that had come to visit Whitewharf a month prior.

Walton simply goggled at the man and even as Gorden Nightshade III approached him on spindly legs, the boy could only watch.

Gorden Nightshade was so tall that Walton could've had another boy on his shoulders and they still wouldn't have reached the oddly proportioned man's chest. Bending at the waist, Gorden Nightshade brought his head down to Walton's level and ran a gloved hand through Walton's thin black hair. The sensation made the boy think of all the times he'd woken to a rat crawling across him in the middle of the night, only all over his body.

"You, dear boy, are very special," Gorden Nightshade told him.

Walton shook his head. "No sir, I'm just the son of the town gravedigger. I've never done anything of import in my life."

116

The smile on the man's face, which seemed to be painted on, grew bigger. His teeth were too large. Everything about the man was wrong. He was more like a thing wearing a man suit. "Yet, my boy!" he exclaimed. "*Yet*." Then, the man-thing that called itself Gorden Nightshade stood upright and held out an arm almost as long as Walton was tall (it seemed he grew more unnatural by the moment). "Now, let's go. There is work to be done."

Walton stared at Gorden's white, gloved hand then looked up at the man. His eyes were vortexes. They were hypnotic.

"I...I don't want to go with you."

"And why would you stay, dear boy? Aside from those buried here, what do you have? A father who hates you? Who beats you? A town full of people that wouldn't piss on you to put you out if you were on fire? Don't be stu-" Gorden Nightshade caught himself, biting his lip in the process with teeth like a wolf's. "Don't be *silly*. Now, come come. We mustn't dally."

Walton knew the man-thing was right but part of him felt like the beatings would be better than whatever this Gorden Nightshade wanted with him. Still, another part wanted to see the world. He took the hand that was offered to him.

It would be ten years before he returned to Whitewharf. Ten years of learning the darkest of magics beneath the watchful eye of the thing that called itself Gorden Nightshade. In those ten years, Gorden Nightshade never revealed to him what he wanted with him, simply assuring Walton that all would be revealed in time.

When Walton Stoneheart came back to Whitewharf, he first paid a visit to the shack he had spent his first twelve years in.

He sat at the foot of his father's bed and waited for him to wake up. When the man finally stirred, he looked shocked to see his son. Walton was surprised Walter even remembered him.

"W-Walton? I thought you were dead. What in the gods' names are you wearing?"

Walton looked down at the red and gold robes Gorden Nightshade had given him. They were special robes, made just for Walton from the finest Arcanian fabrics. Those robes had been the first gift anyone had ever given him. Gorden Nightshade had in those ten years given him *many* gifts.

"Shhh," he told his father as he drove the ornate, black dagger deep into Walter's stomach. The look of shock on the man's face was delicious. Walton watched his father die, noting the man never stopped looking at him, even after he could no longer see.

Once he was gone, Walton brought his father out to the graveyard and tossed his body down. The ceremony had to be performed at sunset, which wasn't for hours. But ten years had passed. Walton had so many things to catch his friends up on.

When the sun began to set, Walton prepared for the ceremony. When the preparation was complete, there were still several minutes left before he had to begin and he spent them standing at the top of the hill overlooking the little hamlet he'd grown up in. All those simple little families living out their simple little lives with no clue of what was fate about to befall them.

When the sun was barely a line across the evening sky, Walton performed his ceremony, just as Gorden Nightshade had taught him. It came easily to him, just as all the other lessons had. It was almost like he had been born to do it.

His father, having not been buried, was the first to rise. Walton smiled. For the first time in his twenty-two years, Walton was the one in control.

He made his father dance as his friends dug themselves out of their graves. Once his little army had been assembled, he gave them their orders. One simple command: "Kill."

And kill they did. By sunrise, the town was a smoldering ruin and his army had grown considerably. Whitewharf was no more. As Walton looked at the devastation he had wrought, he felt a familiar tickle on the back of his neck. Before he could turn around, he heard slow clapping.

"Well done, my boy. I just *knew* you were a natural. Didn't I tell you?"

Walton turned and smiled at his master, who sat perched on a tombstone with a goblet of liquid in his hand. "You certainly did."

"And isn't it nice to see all your old friends again?"

Walton nodded. "It was." Then he asked the logical question: "Now what?"

"Well," the thing in the man-suit replied, "they do say 'practice makes perfect.' Let's take a walk on over to the next town and say hi."

Walton grinned so big it almost matched Gorden Nightshade's.

Decades passed and Walton's power grew and grew. Before long, he had decided that Gorden Nightshade had nothing left to teach him.

Walking up the stairs to the top of the highest tower in the castle they had taken up residence in after slaughtering its occupants years earlier, Walton was prepared for a fight after telling his master that he no longer had any need of him. Upon entering Gorden Nightshade's room in the castle to tell him that he no longer had need of him to find that he knew that their time together had come to an end before Walton did.

On the bed that Walton didn't think had ever once been used was a book bound in the flesh of dark elves. He knew exactly what it was: Gorden Nightshade's grimoire, a book of spells he'd compiled over the countless lifetimes he'd walked amongst the people of Arcania.

There was a note on it: "Use the book wisely, my boy. There is nothing else for me to teach you, so I'm off to find another young boy in need of a friendly but firm hand to guide them. Now, go forth and take what is yours. Your friend GN"

Walton grabbed the book, opened it up, and flipped through it until he found just what he was looking for: instructions for binding his essence to a phylactery in order to attain immortality. The other contents of the book could wait.

Not long after that, he performed the ritual that erased Walton Stoneheart and left in his stead the fearsome, undead necromancer that would in due time be known far and wide simply as the Lich.

With his abilities vastly superior to any other necromancer in the realm, the Lich quickly snuffed out his competition. With none left to challenge him, an army of undead under his command and the grimoire in his possession, only one thing eluded him: the Wellspring. With that under his control, Arcania would only be the first kingdom to fall beneath his skeletal fist. There was an entire universe out there for him to conquer.

Having finished his lengthy trip down memory lane, the Lich found himself looking at a metallic door through the Valkyrie's eyes. The Wellspring lay beyond that door, its power emanating much stronger than elsewhere in the pentagonal keep.

The Lich sent the command to half of the remaining Valkyrie to drop everything and make their way to that door.

He grinned. It wouldn't be long now.

IV.

The General didn't understand it at first when half of the dead women began to turn and walk away. It wasn't exactly a common battle tactic.

"What the hell is going on?" he roared. "Where are they going?"

"Don't know, General, but I think we ought to follow them," Jack told him.

Putting two bullets into a matching set of kneecaps, Wyngarde smirked. "Novel idea, son. Let's finish these harpies off and do just that."

"I have an idea," Tom, the kid who'd blown a giant hole in the wall of the Pentagon, said. "But it'll be messy."

The General knew just what he was thinking. "In any other situation I'd tell you that you were crazy, but this isn't any other situation. Make it rain, son."

"What are you talking about?" the stranger with the sword asked.

"Things are about to get loud, miss. I suggest you cover your ears."

Fwump-BOOM! A sizable chunk of the remaining enemies blew to pieces as the kid shot a grenade at them. Albert winced. He was no stranger to explosions but you never really did get used to it.

"This world is full of wonders," the woman said as she resumed her razor-sharp onslaught.

Tom fired off two more shots from the 'noob tube,' as the General's grandson referred to it, and turned two more chunks of the corpses into, well, chunks of corpse. The half who remained had been reduced to just a few and the combined force of the living made quick work of the dead.

For a rag-tag team of desk workers, they didn't make a bad team.

"Lady, I don't know who you are and we don't exactly have time to make introductions, but I sure am glad you're here to help," Wyngarde informed the newcomer.

"My name is Marjorie Lenoir and I'm from the same place as these monsters," she said, gesturing to the scattered pieces of undead warrior women.

"Yeah, great. Now let's go see what these zombie bitches want with us, huh?"

"Actually, they're not zombies," Marjorie Lenoir informed him. "They're the Valkyrie, animated corpses controlled by the Lich. Zombies are autonomous, operating on pure instinct."

The General looked at her. "Lady, don't take this the wrong way, but I really do not give a flying fuck if they were all fucked-up clones of Patsy Kline. All that matters is we stop them."

The look on the woman's face made it clear that she did not know who Patsy Kline was but understood his sentiment.

"Now, let's go find out what these things came here for, huh?"

As General Wyngarde led his troops to war, he found himself smiling. He almost felt young again.

V.

Alex could tell that June was doing her best to be brave, but it was clear that the girl was terrified. She wished she knew what to do to help the poor kid but her people skills barely extended to adults, never mind an eleven-year-old.

'Socially awkward' wasn't the term she preferred but it was the one that fit Alex the best. She had always been shy and introverted, a child of privilege whose parents were both too wrapped up in their own lives to notice that their daughter wasn't necessarily developing as she maybe should have been.

Instead, when Alex was June's age, she'd get off the bus and walk home to an empty house, make herself a bowl of ice cream (oftentimes that would end up being her dinner), and plop herself in front of the television to watch Toonami and binge watch her older brother's old *Akira* and *Vampire Hunter D* tapes for hours until one of her parents finally came home and shooed her off to bed.

Somewhere deep down, she knew it wasn't their fault. Charlie's death had impacted all of them in different ways. He'd died in Iraq, the victim of a suicide bombing in a little coffee shop he and several of his fellow soldiers were patronizing.

For Alex, she withdrew deep inside her shell and wouldn't really come out for most of middle school and high school. Before he joined the army, she and Charlie would watch anime every Friday night. It never seemed to bother her brother that he was staying in and hanging out with his baby sister while all of his friends were out partying and smoking pot. So, when the soldiers came to their doorstep and handed her mother that flag, the first thing Alex did was walk upstairs into Charlie's room and take all of his VHS tapes. She watched them religiously, over and over again; her own way of keeping her memories of him alive.

For her parents, though, they withdrew in a different way. Even though it was Charlie who had died, Alex's parents may as well have been ghosts. They both seemed so listless; floating from room to room in a fog that lasted years.

But it didn't bother Alex. She was a smart kid and did well in school. She blended in, never exhibited any behavior to suggest that she was virtually raising herself. In the busy District of Columbia school system, there were just too many kids for anybody to notice that one spent all her lunches in the library reading manga by herself.

High school was a little easier for Alex. She had some friends, mostly boys who would go on to become Internet trolls and Men's Rights Activists, but nobody that she still kept in touch with (largely because they'd become Internet trolls and Men's Rights Activists). Having missed out on much of the usual girl stuff growing up, Alex didn't have a lot of female friends. However, there was one girl that Alex would *never* forget.

Her name was Milla and she was one of the most beautiful beings to ever walk the earth. She was tall and fair-skinned with a pixie cut, big pouty lips, and a beauty mark in the exact same spot as Cindy Crawford. Her father was some important government guy from Finland who had moved his family to the states for one reason or another. It was really hard for Alex to retain much of anything Milla had told her during their first encounter.

It was Alex's sophomore year at Lyndon B. Johnson High. She was reading *Berserk* volume three and eating peanut butter crackers in the library just like every day at lunchtime when a shadow fell over her. She looked up and there was Milla, bathed in light. For Alex, it was love at first sight. She'd always wondered why she'd never felt any attraction to any of the boys at school but at that moment the answer was abundantly clear.

"Hello. May I sit?"

Alex was flabbergasted, simply staring at the beautiful and slightly masculine girl that stood in front of her.

"Oh, how rude of me, I am sorry! My name is Milla. I am new here, from Helsinki." Then, she extended a hand.

"Hi," Alex said, taking the other girl's hand in hers and silently marveling at the silky smoothness of it. "Uh, I'm Alex?"

"Are you?"

"Am I what?"

Milla smiled and Alex felt something stirring deep inside her for the first time. "Are you Alex? You said it like a question. I am making a joke."

"Oh! Oh, I get it. Ha." Alex felt very flustered. She already had a hard time people-ing, but lobbing Ms. Finland 2005 at her hardly seemed fair.

"So, may I sit?" Milla asked her again.

"Oh, yes, please, certainly, yes."

Milla sat. "What are you reading?"

Alex held up her book. "It's called *Berserk*. It's about-"

"A very, very angry man named Guts, yes? I love *Berserk*! Have you seen the anime?"

Under the table, Alex pinched herself to make sure she wasn't dreaming. Judging from the pain, she was not. "Y-yeah. I have a bunch of the tapes at home."

"Oh, how fun! Maybe we can watch them some time!"

Alex was completely floored. She contemplated pinching herself again, but instead simply nodded. "S-sure! I'm free this weekend."

"Very good! This weekend it is. Do you have *Akira* too?"

"Do I!?"

Their conversation lasted throughout the rest of lunch when they found themselves forced to return to the humdrum world of school before the late bell rang. But that afternoon when school let out, Alex was surprised to see Milla waiting for her in front of a black town car. The beautiful girl waved as Alex walked over.

"Would you like a ride home, Alex?"

Alex smiled, tucked a strand of hair behind her ear, and nodded.

Getting attached to Milla happened very fast. By the time that Friday rolled around, she was absolutely smitten with the girl. Her hand trembled as she unlocked the door to her house, a thousand different thoughts rushing through her head.

"Where are your parents?" Milla asked her as they walked inside the dark house.

Alex shrugged. "I don't know. They kind of just do their thing, y'know?"

Milla nodded. "Yes, it is the same with Papa."

"So, what do you want to do first?"

Milla looked at her and smiled. "I was actually thinking that maybe we could go up to your room."

"And do what?"

Milla blushed, "Come now, Alex, do not make me say it."

Alex was lost. "Say what? All the video games and stuff are down here."

The other girl shook her head and then, before she knew it, Alex was experiencing her first kiss. On instinct, her hands found purchase on Milla's perfect neck. Backpacks were dropped on the ground and the two girls, joined at the lips, awkwardly made their way upstairs.

And so began Alex's first relationship. It was perfect, as far as first relationships went. Milla's dad took an immediate shine to his daughter's girlfriend and Alex's parents barely even noticed that their daughter had a friend over all the time. The two got along like gangbusters and Alex no longer found herself eating peanut butter crackers alone in the library.

Sadly, like all good things, their relationship came to an end when Milla's father's business in DC finished that summer and Milla had to go back to Helsinki. The two had a very tearful goodbye, but both were realistic about the situation.

The last two years of high school and most of her college experience came and went without much incident and Alex could barely even remember how she ended up majoring in Human Resources Management. Since the course load was pretty easy for her, most of Alex's free time was spent watching anime, reading manga and maintaining a position on the board of the university's Anime Club. She graduated with a 3.9 and a very sexy Finish guardian angel pulled some strings for her and she found herself working in the HR department for the United States Department of Defense! It was a fairly easy job for her as most everyone at the Pentagon knew how to behave themselves, so her days were mostly spent of *Bleach* roleplaying forums and streaming sites.

Nothing that she had experienced at any point, however, prepared her for babysitting an eleven-year-old girl during an invasion of shambling corpse-women.

Alex looked at June, who was staring vacantly off into the distance, sniffling absentmindedly. She then remembered she had her emergency stash on her phone. A smile spread across trembling lips.

"Hey June?"

Another sniffle. The girl looked at her, eyes big and puffy with tears and fear. "Y-yeah?"

"Have you ever watched *Sailor Moon*?"

The girl shook her head. "No, what's that?"

Alex patted the empty chair next to hers. "Why don't you come over here and I'll show you?"

"Okay."

As June walked over, Alex felt a small swelling of pride in her chest. She might not be great at people, but she may have just nailed it with this one.

VI.

Once the banging began, Senator Laura Powers was certain that her time had come.

The Senator, still foggy from the vodka, sat in her chair and sighed. Maybe she deserved it. Maybe all the clandestine business dealing with other dimensions, other realities, was wrong. Maybe the Department of Immigration Studies shouldn't have kept it to themselves.

Now she had to live with the fact, albeit not for much longer in all likelihood, that all those people upstairs had been trapped in the building with no rescue because of her. She'd sent the message declaring it a false alarm. She'd kept the highly-trained soldiers that knew how to kill a man a hundred different ways before they hit the ground from storming the Pentagon and taking out whatever those things out there were.

Lamenting the fact that she was out of booze, Laura's thoughts turned to that fateful night when she met the men that would forever alter the trajectory of her life. If it hadn't been for that piece of shit cheating husband of hers, she never would've been at the reflecting pool when that...that *thing* came through.

The regret tasted bitter in her mouth.

The Senator stood up and walked over to the soldier by the door who looked like he was about to start openly weeping.

"What's your name, son?" she asked him, her words only slurring ever so slightly.

"Evan Clark," he said, his voice quaking.

"Evan my boy, do you have any regrets?"

The soldier thought on it, then nodded. "I never asked Frankie Noonan out in high school and she ended up getting married to this asshole Scott Nutterman right after graduation. We, we called him Scott Nutterbutter."

Senator Powers smirked. "Are you afraid to die, Evan?"

The boy stared at her for several long moments, then nodded. "Yes ma'am, I am."

"Well then are you ready to fight to keep that from happening?"

"I-I-I suppose I am, ma'am."

The smirk turned to a smile. "Good boy." She patted him on the shoulder and turned to all the other so-called 'Very Important People' in the safe room. "How about you all, hmm? Are you ready to fight for your lives or are you going to just lay down and take it?"

A Democratic member of the House from somewhere on the West Coast, she couldn't remember where, looked at her. "I'd rather die fighting, personally."

Murmurs of agreement from the other men and women in the room.

Senator Laura Powers walked over to a nondescript wall panel, opened it to reveal a keypad, and entered the code '1-7-7-6.' The wall in front of her raised up to reveal a small arsenal of weapons ranging from the mundane to the more exotic. She picked up a small, hand-held flamethrower and turned to the other people in the room, who all stared at the stockpile of weapons that had been hidden from sight.

Feeling like she was on a roll, the Senator held up a hand. "Before you all choose your instruments of divine retribution, I would like to give to you a snippet from one of my favorite poems: 'Do not go gentle into that good night, old age should burn and rave at close of day; rage, rage against the dying of the light.'" She paused for effect. "Now, let us rage, rage against the dying of the light, shall we?"

VII.

As the sword pierced his stomach, Tom barely felt it. He instinctively pulled the trigger on his rifle and vaporized the head of the Valkyrie that stabbed him, then looked down at the blade. It was serrated, like a giant steak knife. Blood began to flow from the wound and he was surprised to see that instead of his whole life, it was simply the last five minutes flashed through his mind.

They had followed the Valkyrie, giving the apparently remote-controlled creatures a wide berth lest their master detect that they were being followed. The Valkyrie had entered an innocuous-looking doorway (the door itself had been hacked to pieces) into what appeared to be a janitor's closet. A hidden door had been literally peeled open, revealing a passageway that descended down beneath the Pentagon.

"What is this place?" Jefferson had asked.

The General answered the question. It led to a bunker where all the VIPs were taken to when a red alert was triggered.

"So you mean to tell me that while people are dying up here, they're safe and sound in their little air-conditioned safe room?" Jack asked. Tom had always been intimidated by the man. Before the Valkyrie attacked, they'd never said one word to each other, but the pain and sadness he radiated was tangible.

"I was down there, y'know." the General told them. "Didn't sit right with me neither. That's why I came up to fight. And besides, how safe d'you think they feel now with a swarm of these nasty, maggot-riddled bitches knocking on their doors?"

Tom looked at Jack considering the question and couldn't help but grin. The General made an excellent point.

Marjorie, the woman from another world who came out of nowhere to help them fight the Valkyrie, spoke up. "I don't mean to be rude, but should we go and rescue your 'Vee Eye Peas?'"

A nod from the General. "Be careful. The doors may be a good three feet of solid steel but we don't know how much damage they were already able to do. It'd be a shame for one of the big wigs to catch a stray bullet." To Tom, it sounded like maybe Wyngarde didn't 100% mean that.

Before anybody could move, he heard Jefferson shout "LOOK OUT!" but it was too late for Tom to do anything but turn around and meet his maker.

The sword entered him like it was one of those half-heart necklaces that had found its mate, like it and his midsection belonged together. The burst from the assault rifle had knocked that particular Valkyrie away, but two more were on him in a second. How they managed to sneak up behind him and the others, Tom had no clue, but that didn't matter. He was dead.

But if he was going to die, he wasn't going without a fight.

He pressed the rifle to one of his attackers' skulls and aerated it, removing the enemy from his arm, which had a giant chunk missing. Tom swallowed, but his throat was very dry. It was almost time.

"*C'mon son,*" he heard his father tell him. "*You did good. You can let go now.*"

With some small regret that he hadn't been more help to the General and the others, Tom let go.

VIII.

The banging had only increased after the shooting started.

Evan Clark had enrolled into the United States military right out of high school. He had maintained a solid C+ average throughout all of high school and managed to get into a few okay schools but his family was dirt poor and Evan knew that he wasn't exactly going to be qualifying for any of the fancier scholarships or grants any of the schools he'd applied to had to offer.

Rather than get a job ringing up groceries at the Buy-More in town or scooping popcorn at the movie theater, he did like many men and women before him and enlisted.

Boot camp wasn't all that terrible for him. His father spent all eighteen years of Evan's life screaming at him, so the drill sergeants just made him feel at home. Despite his somewhat lanky physique, Evan had found a home on the school track and even made the Varsity squad, although he never brought home any medals (much to his father's chagrin), so all the running and jumping and the dozens of other drills weren't much of an issue either.

The time he spent at boot camp was fairly uneventful and before he knew it, Evan found himself posted in Washington. After a few months manning a post at the Library of Congress, he had been transferred to the Pentagon and for the first three months everything had been great.

Then, some sort of undead nightmare was unleashed and he found himself as one of only two soldiers that were in the underground bunker protecting senators, congressmen, and a few military higher-ups. The other guy, Palmer, was a total tool and sat in the corner playing a cellphone game, somehow able to ignore the fact that zombies were trying to make their way into the bunker.

When the shooting started, hope began to swell in Evan's chest. Maybe, just maybe, they were saved.

Then all at once, the banging *and* the shooting stopped.

"Wh-what happened?" an Asian man in a suit worth more than what Evan would've taken home in a year at the movie theater asked. "Is it over?"

Before anybody could offer up an answer, there was more banging. Someone shrieked. But it wasn't the same kind of banging.

It was somebody knocking on the door to the tune of "Shave and a Haircut."

"There's only one man I know who'd use that knock in the middle of the goddamn zombie apocalypse. Let'm in," the drunk senator from Texas slurred.

Evan punched in the code to the door and it raised. Standing on the other side was General Wyngarde, another white guy, a black guy, and a girl who looked like she had come straight out of a medieval fantasy game. All of them looked like they'd been through hell.

The General, without looking at him, pressed a bloody assault rifle to Evan's chest. "It ain't yours, kid, but it'll do. The other guy ain't using it anymore." Then, he slumped down in the nearest open chair and looked at Senator Powers. "Powers, there's something in here that those things want. I don't know what and I don't know where, but-"

"I do," the Senator told him. It came out as some sort of weird croak.

"*What?*" the General asked, his weary face washing over with shock.

136

The medieval fantasy girl with the red hair stepped forward. "It's the Wellspring." Her statement certainly was not posed as a question.

Senator Powers looked at her. "H-how do you know about that?"

"I come from the realm of Arcania. The Wellspring is the most powerful artifact of our world. It's why the Lich has torn this stronghold to pieces with his Valkyrie. Take me to it. *Now*."

"Listen here, young lady-" the Senator began.

The General stood up. "Powers, do what she says. This isn't the time for any sort of chain-of-command bullshit." Then, a pause. "And don't think you and I won't have a good, long conversation later, lady."

"I...okay. Follow me."

The Senator led the two men and the woman over to a bust a JFK in the corner of the room. She pulled the man's head back to reveal a keyhole. Inserting a key she pulled from her pocketbook, she turned it and another secret chamber stood revealed. It was an elevator.

"After you," she said, letting the three newcomers enter. "Are you coming, Albert?"

The General shook his head. "Nah, I'll stay up here with the string bean and guard the door. I know we didn't get'm all and I'm sure now they're out for blood. And besides, I don't think I could look at you for one more second right now."

"Fine," Senator Powers said flatly, pursing her lips, as she inserted the same key into a panel in the elevator. The doors closed and then they were gone, presumably going down to some secret sub-basement beneath the Pentagon.

Evan clutched the bloody rifle and tried not to look like he'd been crying, hoping the General wouldn't notice.

"Kid," the General said, nearly a grunt.

"Y-yes, sir?"

"Can you get me a beer or a soda or something? I'm dyin' of thirst."

Evan simply nodded and ran to the mini-fridge on the other side of the room. The rest of the VIP's had run a train on it over the last several hours and all that was left was grapefruit Fresca. He handed it to the General.

"It's, it's all they had left."

The General gave him a weary smile as he popped open the can. "It's fine, kid. Relax. I can think of about a dozen worse sodas I could be stuck with in the war against otherworldly necromancers. Hell, it's even the best flavor."

Evan watched the General guzzle the whole thing in one go.

"That's good stuff."

"Did you say 'necromancer,' sir?"

The General nodded, setting his can down on the table. "Some all-powerful sorcerer named the Lich. Sounds like something from *Lord of the Ring.*"

Evan half-smiled. "It's, uh, *Rings*, sir. Plural. The One Ring is just one of nineteen different rings."

"Heh. Excuse me, my apologies to Mr. Tolkien." The General looked at him and smiled. "How old are you, kid?"

"20, sir."

The General whistled. "Jeez, can't even buy your own alcohol yet but you can certainly defend your country from zombie bitches from Hell." Then, he leaned forward and looked up at Evan. "Listen, uh," he read Evan's fatigues, "Private Clark, we make it out of here? I'm gonna buy you a drink."

Evan's face lit up. "Wow, okay, sure."

"I got a grandson your age. He's into all that fantasy shit too. Took him to see the second or third *Hobbit*, I don't remember which, the one with the Orcs."

Evan smiled. That was all of them, but he kept it to himself. "That's awesome."

"Yeah, the kid even got me to put on elf ears, can you picture it?"

Evan could not.

"God, I hope I make it out of here," the General said, displaying a sudden vulnerability that took Evan completely by surprise. "I got four grandkids between my son and daughter and all I want is to see them again. Hell, I'll put the whole damn elf costume on next time."

Tempting fate, Evan put a hand on the General's arm. "We're going to get out of here, sir. We're going to have that beer and I'm going to see you in that elf costume."

The General, his eyes glossy, smiled. "Private Clark, you'd better make that two beers."

139

IX.

The Lich was not happy.

And when he wasn't happy, he got angry.

To vent his frustrations, he had one of the skeletons bring him a black Goob to take his frustrations out on. They were incredibly hard-to-kill creatures made of a barely-sentient ooze and as such, made for excellent tools for anger management.

As he pummeled the gelatinous blob, the Lich thought about his next course of action. There were only two Valkyrie left with fully-functioning bodies. The good news was the less of them he had to control, the more control he had over each one. The others had been rendered useless so quickly that he hadn't been able to appreciate that fact, but these last few would prove to be incredibly deadly.

Despite how deadly those last two Valkyrie would prove to be, the likelihood that they would be able to get their skeletal talons on the Wellspring before the humans rendered their bodies useless was slim, and if he ran out of usable Valkyrie, that left only one option. Despite his nearly-limitless power, it was still an incredibly risky plan.

But he would cross that bridge, burn it to the ground, scatter the ashes to the winds, find the architect of said bridge, make him watch as the life drained from his family, and then drink him dry when he got to it.

X.

The elevator felt like it had been descending forever. Jefferson was growing impatient. All he wanted in the world was for the horror show his life had become over the past few hours to end so he could hug his daughter for about a week.

At least he knew she was safe. Marjorie, thank whatever gods were listening, had seen to that.

"So, what exactly is down in this secret sub-basement that the Lich wants so badly?" he asked, breaking the silence.

The senator, who smelled like the expensive kind of vodka he ordered when he was trying to impress women at the bar, looked at him with glassy, red eyes. "The Wellspring. It's a, it's a, powerful magic artifact of incredible magical power."

Jefferson fought the impulse to roll his eyes. Before he could ask a follow-up about this 'Wellspring,' Marjorie beat him to the punch.

"How did the Wellspring get to this realm?" She seemed gravely concerned.

Senator Powers' face took on a scowl and her slurring decreased dramatically. "A warlock brought it here. 'Dran the Clever,' he called himself. Helped us make the room I'm taking you two to. He...he said he'd come back, but...he never did."

The concern only increased on Marjorie's face. "That's because he's dead."

'Crestfallen' was the only word to describe the look that replaced the scowl on the Senator's face. "Oh," she said, almost a whisper.

The monster hunter shook her head. "No, I'm afraid you misunderstand me, madam. Dran the Clever died a century ago in battle with the Dragon Lord."

A hand raised to the Senator's mouth. She looked shocked.

Jack, who had been listening intently for the duration of the weirdly-long elevator ride, asked the logical question: "So if this Dran the Clever guy has been dead this whole time then who the hell brought the Wellspring here?"

Marjorie slowly shook her head. "I do not know, but it is certainly cause for concern."

Just then, the elevator stopped. Jefferson hadn't realized he'd been holding his breath, but he finally let it out. As the door opened, he felt an instant change. Everything suddenly felt electric.

There was magic in the air.

XI.

Sailor Moon had just killed the fortune teller monster when Alex's phone died. While the anime had worked wonders to keeping her distracted, now that it was gone all the terror came back with a vengeance. June gritted her teeth and felt fresh, hot tears welling up in her eyes.

"Maybe I can find a phone charger," Alex offered, standing up.

June shook her head. "No, it's okay," she said, following the statement with a liberal sniffle. "Do you think that my dad is okay?"

The woman smiled at her and nodded. "Your father makes Tuxedo Mask look like a wussy. I'm sure he's like, five minutes away from saving the day."

Despite the fear in Alex's voice, June could tell that she meant what she said. It made the girl feel much better.

"Have you ever played MASH, Alex?"

"Nope, what's that?"

The girl beamed and grabbed a piece of paper and a pen from the desk she was sitting at and ran over to the one that Alex was sitting at. "It's like getting your fortune told, kind of? Jenny Hurst showed me in homeroom. Here, I'll show you!"

"Sounds good to me," the woman said with a big grin.

June liked Alex a lot and she bet Marjorie would too, once she and her dad were done murderizing the Lich.

The eleven-year-old grinned and began to explain how the game worked to her friend.

XII.

"Marjorie? Can you hear me?" a familiar disembodied voice said in Marjorie's mind as she followed her fellows-in-arms and the old woman in the strange pink outfit down the long, metal hallway.

The woman couldn't help but grin. "Yes, I'm here."

The other three turned and looked at her and Marjorie felt warmth in her cheeks.

"Oh, uh," she fumbled for the words, feeling very much like the inexperienced girl that had entered the Lich's castle earlier that day, "My sword is host to a legendary monster hunter named Arthur d'Argetan. It's not uncommon to have spirits bound to weapons or armor where I come from."

Jack, who had beautiful ebony skin the likes of which that Marjorie had never seen before, smirked. "Yeah, that scales. After the day I've had, I wouldn't be surprised to find out that you can shoot fireballs out of your ass."

Looking to regain some ground with her compatriots, Marjorie grinned and decided to show off, producing a flame from her pointer finger. "I do not own an ass, but I can make my own flames."

The man opened his mouth to reply, then just grinned and shook his head.

"Would you all like to stand around and swap recipes all day or would you maybe like to continue to the Room of Wards and figure out how best to stop this Lich of yours?" the Senator asked.

Marjorie liked this Senator Laura Powers. She reminded her of her father, Bartholomew. A fan of the drink, a biting wit, and fiercely capable, he was the first of the Lenoir monster hunters to challenge the Lich in hopes of bringing an end to his reign of terror and liberating their kingdom from the monster's cold, undead hands.

Her father was also the first of the Lenoirs to make his debut as a head on a pike outside the Lenoir home. Jasper, the second-youngest member of the Lenoir children, told her that it was a good thing their mother had already died, as such a ghastly site would surely have done the same job that the Wintersick had. At least with the Wintersick, she had gone peacefully.

James was next to challenge the Lich. He was the eldest and every bit the monster hunter his father had been and he felt it that it was his duty to avenge their father. The Lich sent him back to them as a zombie. Connor, the second-oldest and handiest with ranged weaponry, put an arrow right between his brother's eyes.

However, Connor's expertise with the bow and arrow would not prevent him from returning home in pieces, stacked like a grotesque parody of a burial cairn. A simple note written in shockingly ornate calligraphy was pinned to his forehead, nestled in the center of the pile. It read simply, "Who's next?"

That very same night, Jasper took up sword and shield and made his way to the castle even as his sister, the only family he had to leave behind, begged and pleaded with him not to go.

"I must, sister," he told her, his face set in stone. "That monster has killed our father and our brothers. He must pay." Then, Jasper kissed her forehead and left her behind. The next time she would see him, he would be ashes in an urn.

145

Marjorie found herself all alone in the world. With her father and brothers gone, she sank into a deep depression. Days passed without her leaving her bed. When she finally did, she had her mind set on joining them all in the afterlife.

She stood in her father's armory and picked his favorite sword. When it spoke to her, she practically dropped the blade. Her father had never mentioned that Finem was host to one of the greatest monster hunters in all of Arcania.

D'Argetan made her a promise: if she would promise him not to give up, he would help her become a monster hunter in her own right and teach her the skills she needed to challenge the Lich.

Weeks passed in a blur as Marjorie trained her body and mind for what laid in wait for her in the monster's castle. She knew it was probably a suicide mission, but at least she would die with honor.

The fear she'd felt as she stood in front of the Lich's castle was still so fresh in her mind. It felt like years had passed by but it had only been mere *hours* since she had entered the castle. Now she was in another world, about to find herself face-to-face with the most powerful artifact in all of Arcania.

"It's okay to be afraid, child," d'Argetan said, echoing his statement from earlier that day when Marjorie stood before the entrance to the Lich's fortress, a scared girl full of trepidation.

Coming to a stop before the door to the Room of Wards, a small smile crept across Marjorie's lips. "I'm not scared, d'Argetan, and I'm not a child. Not anymore."

XIII.

The first Fresca was gone. General Wyngarde was on his second. The crisp, refreshing Grapefruit-flavored beverage did little for his mood but at least he was hydrated.

For the first time in a long time, the General felt all sixty-eight of his years. It had been a long, long time since he'd seen active duty and now that the adrenaline wasn't pumping so quickly, the last few hours began to catch up with him.

"Are you alright, sir?" the kid asked him.

He gave the boy a wan smile. "Just tired, son. When you're my age, killing zombies takes a lot more out of you than it used to. Now, tell me again how we stop the Lich?"

Evan smiled, clearly glad to be able to put his wealth of knowledge to good use, and told the General, "Every Lich has a phylactery, which is basically its Horcrux, like from *Harry Potter?*"

The General shrugged.

"It's like, it's the thing that powers the Lich, keeps him from turning to dust. You destroy it or cut him off from it and he's done."

"Hm. That simple, huh?"

Evan opened his mouth to respond when the bunker trembled. People screamed and Wyngarde felt his teeth grinding. Something was happening up top and he knew that it had to do with that godforsaken portal to wherever it was that the Valkyrie came from.

"Is it an earthquake?" someone asked.

147

The General ignored the question and stood. Evan looked at him.

"Sir?"

"We need to get up there, kid."

"Shouldn't we wait for-"

Another tremble. The General looked at him. "I don't think that's an option." He put a hand on Evan's shoulder. "Are you with me?"

Evan saluted him. "Sir, yes sir."

Wyngarde turned to the other soldier, the dickhead that was too busy on his fucking cell phone to even look up when the underground bunker he was in began to shake. "What's his name, soldier?"

"Palmer, sir."

"HEY! PALMER!" the General shouted.

The soldier looked up, saw the General staring daggers at him, and shot right up out of his chair. "Sir!"

"Fall in."

"Yes sir!"

As Palmer trotted over, Wyngarde looked at the impressive array of guns that had been hidden in the bunker. One in particular caught his eye: a long, chrome, shotgun-like weapon. Whatever it was, it wasn't standard issue. He picked it up and felt a small vibration.

Out of curiosity, he took aim at the far wall and pulled the gun's trigger. A purple beam shot out and vaporized a chunk of wall, revealing the earth behind it.

"Yeah, this'll do jussssssssst fine."

Then, the General scanned the room. "Any of you pencil-necks have a Sharpie?"

A Hispanic woman in a suit that probably cost more than the kid made in three months nodded and pulled one out of her purse. The General took it, walked over to the bunker door, and left a message for Brody and the others. Once that was done, he tossed the marker back to its owner and turned to the two soldiers. "You boys ready?"

"Sir!" they said in unison.

"Hooah," the General said, heading for the bunker door.

XIV.

Having taking several moments to reassess his situation, it became clear to the Lich that both of his remaining Valkyrie were too far away from the Wellspring to be of any real use, and that meant it was indeed time for Plan B. After all, if you wanted a job done right, it was always better to do it yourself.

Leaving his phylactery unattended was risky, but taking it with him was even riskier. And now that the Wellspring stood revealed, it would not remain unattended for long.

With a grin, the Lich took his favorite staff, Deathbringer, down from its place above his throne. Deathbringer had been carved from the bones of a great and powerful witch priestess, stained with the blood of the Unicorn King and embedded with one of the two Orbs of Eldon, the notorious Fallen Prince.

With a parting glance at his phylactery, the Lich stepped through the portal and into the other world. Godhood was so close he could taste it.

XV.

Stepping into the Room of Wards was like stepping into some kind of museum. Jack found himself mystified by all the magical artifacts contained within it, but it was the orb that sat on a velvet pillow under glass covered in golden runes that kept drawing his eye.

It generated a golden light that bathed the smoke churning around within. It was beautiful, hypnotic.

"You must destroy it, Jack." A chill ran down Jack's spine when he heard Bethany's voice. He closed his eyes and counted to ten just like the shrink had taught him to do whenever he felt himself slipping.

Just as he'd hit ten, she spoke again. *"Please, Jack, you must destroy the Wellspring."* His late wife's voice was as mesmerizing as it had been in life, deftly penetrating all of his defenses.

He opened his eyes and saw Jefferson staring at him. "You alright, Gramps?"

"Yeah," Jack said, trying to smile and failing spectacularly, "I'm fine."

Jefferson nodded slowly, very clearly unconvinced. "Alright, if you say so. Just keep it together."

When he felt the ginger touch of her fingers on his cheek, Jack felt like he might scream. He was losing his mind or some magic hunk of junk in the room was messing with it.

"You're not imagining it, Jack. I'm really here." He turned and there was Bethany. Sort of.

She was a shimmering, translucent blue apparition floating right in front of his eyes by the entrance to the room. She wore a simple sundress just like she had in the summer when they'd go on picnics. He'd always loved her in a sundress.

Bethany smiled at him. "*If you destroy it, then nobody can use its power for evil.*"

The ghost of his wife made a very compelling point.

"*Please, Jack. If the Lich gets a hold of the Wellspring, the world as we know it is over.*"

Jack turned to see the women carefully lifting the glass case that protected the Wellspring off of the podium it rested on. He was sure they'd come up with a plan, but he hadn't heard a word of it. Bethany's voice had his undivided attention.

His Glock felt hot against his chest. He had a clear shot.

"*Do it, Jack.*"

Before he could act, Marjorie stood before him. "She's not real, Jack."

"Wh-what?"

"I can't hear what she's saying to you, but I can see the woman floating behind you. It's a trick. The Wellspring wants to be released and it will worm its way into the weakest mind in the room to manipulate them into granting its wish."

Jack shook his head. "No, you're wrong. Why...what? How do you know? Did your talking sword tell you?"

Marjorie nodded. "If you were to destroy the Wellspring, it would release its magic into this world and there would be chaos."

"She's lying, Jack. She just wants you for herself."

Before he could argue with the woman from the other world, everything trembled around them. The suit of armor in the corner rattled, the scythe on the wall clacked against the hooks keeping it suspended, and the podium the Wellspring sat atop threatened to fall. Jefferson stepped in and held it steady.

"What was that?" Senator Powers asked.

Jack saw how pale the girl had suddenly become and knew that it whatever caused the tremors was nothing good.

"The Lich...he's crossed over."

"Destroy the Wellspring, Jack, before it's too late."

"What...what's the plan?" Jack asked.

After being sufficiently sure that the tremors were over, Jefferson released the podium and looked at Jack. "We're going to get this thing back to the other side and destroy it, releasing it there, where it belongs. The Lich being on this side...complicates things."

"So what do we do?"

Marjorie drew her talking sword. "What else is there to do? We fight."

"Destroy the Wellspring, Jack. Release me."

He tried to block Bethany out. "Then we fight. But there's one more issue, ladies and gents."

"What's that?" Senator Powers asked.

Jack made a sweeping arm across the room. "We're standing in a secret room full of magical bullshit that some *other* magical demon king or whatever could come looking for. We need to destroy it."

The Senator nodded. "You're...not wrong. We built a self-destruct sequence for just that occasion."

"Who's 'we,' Senator?" Jefferson asked.

The woman ignored him as she went to a panel on the wall, opened it revealing a keypad, and entered a chain of eight numbers then hit a big red button.

"Let's be off, children. We've got two minutes before this place is toast."

Jack watched as Jefferson took the Wellspring and tucked it into one of his pockets like someone would a cell phone. He and Powers made for the door. Marjorie, on the other hand, walked over to the wall and took the nasty-looking scythe from the wall. "What are you doing with that?" Jefferson asked her.

The girl smiled. "It just seems like such a shame to let such a beautiful weapon go to waste."

"A minute and a half, boys and girls!" the Senator yelled from down the hall.

Jack and Marjorie rushed out of the room, with Jack taking one last look back to see if Bethany was still there. She was, floating there, watching him go.

"It's not really her, Jack," Marjorie reassured him as they got in the elevator.

154

"I know, I know, it was just...nice to see her again."

The doors shut and the elevator began to ascend.

"I lost my family too," Marjorie told him. "The Lich killed them all. I'd come to his castle to try and get revenge for my father and brothers. I believe fate brought me there on this day for a reason."

Jack chuckled and smiled humorlessly. "Yeah, well, pardon my French but fate can suck my dick."

The look on Marjorie's face was quizzical to say the least. From below them, a muffled explosion could be heard.

As the doors to the elevator opened back into the bunker, Jack cocked his shotgun. "Let's end this."

Act Six:
The Man Comes Around

I.

The pencil-necks from the bunker had followed them. Wyngarde could hardly believe it. For a moment, he'd thought about trying to dissuade them, but if a twenty-year-old kid was willing to lay down his life for his country then the stuffed shirts he'd been charged with protecting could carry their own weight for once.

All of them had armed themselves previously, before he'd made it to the bunker, and the General couldn't help but wonder how many of them had ever even fired a gun before. All the pale, sweaty faces stared at him, searching his face for something, anything.

Closing his eyes, Wyngarde took a deep breath and addressed the group of men and women.

"Okay, look: the fact of the matter is none of you are trained combatants. But that isn't what's important. What is important is that you left that bunker prepared to lay down your lives to beat back the monsters that have killed our friends and loved ones and that shows me that you all are brave. You may not be trained combatants, but I'll be damned if you aren't all soldiers today."

Several people half-smiled and nodded. One woman hugged her rifle to her chest like a security blanket.

"Now, when we get out of here," the General continued, "I'm buying the first round."

He turned towards the exit to the central courtyard, saw the bodies strewn about like unfinished ragdolls, their stuffing more on the outside than in. Ground Zero indeed, he thought with a small frown.

157

Pitch-black storm clouds had gathered over the Pentagon and Wyngarde could see a monstrous figure standing in front of the portal. Visions of those ghost-zombie things from the last *Lord of the Rings* movie flashed through his mind and he thought of Martin. If he didn't stop the Lich, who knows what would happen to his grandson, to *any* of his grandkids. The man shook his head. It was time to end this incursion.

Wyngarde closed his eyes and thought again of his grandchildren. He wished that he'd been able to see them one last time.

Lifting his head up, the General looked at Private Clark. "You ready, kid?"

The boy looked at him, fear plastered across his face like a scarlet letter. "Yes, sir," he said, voice cracking, "as I'll ever be."

Wyngarde smiled. "Good." He turned to the Very Important People that had decided to join him in what he knew at the end of the day was a suicide mission. He smiled at them, hoping it was as cocksure as he meant it to be. "Let's make it hot, folks! Let's show this undead son of a bitch that you don't fuck with America!"

People cheered. Feeling like a much younger man, the General kicked open the door to the courtyard.

Men and women in suits and ties and cardigans ran forth to fight an unknown enemy. Despite the giant ball of dread in his stomach, the General couldn't help but feel a little proud.

Then, as an eldritch blast put a hole where his chest had been, all that General Albert Yancy Wyngarde could feel was cold.

And I heard, as it were, the noise of thunder: One of the four beasts saying: "Come and see." And I saw. And behold, a white horse.

158

Laying on what little remained of his back, the old soldier stared up at the black storm clouds, not really seeing them, and thought of Martin and the time they went out on the boat. It had just been the two of them, and they'd spent the whole day on the

II.

"*June,*" a voice whispered.

June looked around, but it was just her and Alex still. She felt funny all of a sudden, like she did when she had food poisoning that time and threw up on Carter Sinclair in art class in third grade. But it wasn't food poisoning.

It was worse.

"*Listen to me, June. Your father needs you,*" it told her. "*You need to help him destroy the Wellspring.*"

June wasn't sure what the Wellspring was, but she could tell that the voice was telling the truth. She didn't know how and she didn't know why, but she knew that it was.

"Are you okay, June?" Alex asked her, the concern evident on her face.

June stood up. "My dad's in trouble," she said, surprised at how hoarse her voice sounded all of a sudden.

"What?"

"*You need to help him, June,*" the voice told her.

"I need to help him!" June said as made for the door.

"June, stop!" Alex cried as she stood and went to restrain the girl.

June shoved the woman back with such force that she fell back onto her butt.

With Alex out of the way, the girl threw open the door.

I'm coming, Daddy, she thought to herself.

With no previous knowledge of the layout of the Pentagon, June deftly made her way to the central courtyard.

III.

When they stepped out of the elevator, Jefferson had been both surprised and unnerved to see that the bunker stood empty. What had happened that would cause everyone to leave the relative safety of the bunker for whatever was still outside?

"What's the hell is a phylactery?" Jack asked, stirring Jefferson from his thoughts.

He looked in Jack's direction and saw that somebody had left a message for them, written in permanent marker, on the bunker door.

It read: NO PHYLACTERY = NO LICH

Whoever had written it, presumably the General, had clearly done it in a hurry.

"A phylactery is a magical container that stores a Lich's soul. If we destroy it, or even cut off access to it, then the Lich would be no more."

Jefferson nodded. "So, kind of like a back-up Hail Mary for our Hail Mary."

"Once again I do not understand your reference, but I think I understand your sentiment. Yes, if I for some reason cannot get the Wellspring back to Arcania to destroy it, then severing the Lich's connection from his phylactery will bring my quest for vengeance to an end."

"Speaking of your quest for vengeance, I wanted to run an idea by you before we rush off to our deaths all willy-nilly, Marjorie," Jack said.

"Yes?"

"What if you stayed here and let someone else take the Wellspring back to Arcania?"

Jefferson and Marjorie both spoke in unison: "What?"

Jack ran a hand over his short, black hair. "You said so yourself, you don't have any family back there. I don't have any here. I used to be a goddamn CIA agent and now I post pictures of cats on fucking Facebook." The look on Marjorie's face told Jefferson that most of what Jack was saying was going over her head, but the man continued undaunted. "Provided we actually make it through this alive, we'd both have a fresh start. An opportunity to leave our ghosts behind."

Jefferson hadn't seen many sides of Jack before. Previously, he was fairly certain the man only possessed Irritated, Angry, and Stoic. In that moment, the look on the man's face was Sincere, Heartbroken, and Earnest all at once.

"Gramps..." he started.

Jack ignored him, keeping his gaze on the girl from another world. "Just an idea."

Jefferson turned to Marjorie. She stood there for a moment, then handed Jack her sword, a smile on her face. "If you're going to Arcania, you'll need a guide. D'Argetan will tell you everything you'll need to know."

"Once again, a very tender moment, but don't you three have a magical artifact and an undead necromancer to tend to?" Senator Powers asked from the seat she'd taken upon their return from the sub-basement.

"You aren't coming?" Jefferson asked.

She smiled, but it was bereft of any happiness. "Don't take this the wrong way, but I'm too important to die here today." She paused. "No matter how much I may deserve it. This world depends on me just as much as it depends on you right now, and I have nothing to offer you up there."

Jack scoffed but said nothing.

"Well then, I guess we'll see you on the other side," Jefferson said.

Another smile, less cold than the previous one. "I certainly hope so, Mr. Brody. The code to the bunker door is '0216.' Good luck."

They made their way to the bunker door. Before Jefferson punched in the key code, he turned to Jack. "I'm gonna miss you, Gramps."

Jack gave him a sad smile. "Don't worry, kid. I'll send you a postcard."

Then, the man hugged him, which took Jefferson by complete surprise. After moment, he hugged him back.

"Alright," Jack said as he pulled away, "now that we're done 'swapping recipes,' I do believe we have a lich to slay."

Jefferson entered the code on the door's keypad and the door opened. "Well, here goes nothing."

IV.

It was close now and coming closer with every moment. The Lich could feel it. The Wellspring was so powerful that it enabled magic on this side of the portal. The Lich took full advantage of that, easily disposing of the pitiful excuse of a resistance that threw themselves at him, and once he was done with that, he uttered a few words in a long-dead language and the resistance got back up. Zombies were nowhere near as effective as the Valkyrie, but they could move on their own and would serve the twin purposes of occupying any further opposition and growing their ranks while he retrieved the Wellspring and became a dark god more powerful than any that had come before him.

He was so close he could taste it.

And ascension tasted sweet.

V.

"You sure you don't need the sword, kid?" Jack asked Marjorie as they prepared their final assault.

The monster hunter held up the scythe she'd taken from the Room oif Wards. "This will suit me just fine. And so long as the Wellspring is on this side, I have full access to my magic." Then, she looked out at the courtyard, saw that the many victims of the Valkyrie and their master had risen as the shambling undead, and grunted. "I don't suppose you have access to a nearby Save Room, do you?"

"A what?"

"Nothing, never mind. Are you two ready?"

Neither man looked ready, but both nodded.

"Then let us bring this quest to an end."

Jefferson cocked his shotgun. "Yes, let's."

With that, Marjorie, just a scared girl hours earlier, led the two men to battle against her nemesis.

VI.

Evan was hiding in the Ground Zero café, clutching the General's laser rifle thing, when the dead rose.

Once he saw the General go down, he ran. He hated himself for it, but it was like he wasn't in control of his body. He took shelter in the café and waited for the screams and gunfire to stop.

It was worse when they did.

Evan didn't move a muscle. He had hidden in the manager's office, despite the door being completely destroyed. The office was simply the furthest point from the entrance to the café and to the rattled young man, it seemed like it made the most sense. It wasn't until after he'd settled in that he saw the body. It was the café's assistant manager, Tammy. Her throat had been shredded and she laid there in a congealed pool of her own blood, dead eyes staring at the ceiling.

"Fuck," he whispered, sliding down against the wall.

As if the traumatic events Evan had been living through weren't bad enough, the Senator had stirred up some feelings he thought he'd finally buried. Frankie Noonan, Jesus Christ. He hadn't thought of her in months. Now, it felt like his heart was breaking all over again.

It was bad enough that she ended up marrying Nutterbutter right out of high school, but for him to walk away scot-free after the car accident that took her life hardly seemed fair. Not even married for two months and Nutterbutter overestimated his tolerance for alcohol, took a turn too quickly on their way home from some going-away-to-college bonfire, wrecked his nice, shiny sports car Daddy gave him for graduation, and killed the love of Evan's life instantly.

Trying to forget is what led Evan to join the army in the first place. It took time, but eventually his heart stopped hurting as much. 'What if I'd asked her to prom?' It was that terrible What If that haunted him, along with all of the questions that came after it: What if she said yes? What if we had a great time? What if she dated me instead of him? Would she still be alive?

He'd finally put it all behind him several months ago and now it was back in full force.

It wasn't until Tammy was standing right over him that Evan was brought back to reality.

The former assistant manager of the Ground Zero café did not look well, largely due to the gaping hole in her throat. She looked down at him, her jaw working open and down ever so slightly as if she was trying to say something.

Evan found himself frozen in place. Unlike General Wyngarde and the others, he hadn't seen any of the corpse-women in person so staring down the walking corpse of the woman he'd just bought a mediocre coffee from two days prior was a new and terrifying experience for him.

When the dead woman reached out for him, his training kicked in. He lifted the weird silver rifle and pulled the trigger. Tammy's head ceased to exist and the rest of her body dropped back down to the ground.

Evan's breath caught in his chest. "Jesus fucking shit," he cursed. Tears began to stream down his face and he let out one guttural sob.

"*It's okay, Evan*," Frankie told him. The hairs on the back of his neck stood on end and goose bumps broke out over his entire body.

He looked up and there she was, as beautiful as ever, floating where just moments earlier a zombie had stood.

"Fr-Frankie?"

She smiled and nodded. *"It's me, Evan. I've missed you."*

Evan shook his head. "No, it's not you. It's a trick."

"Do you remember when we went to the beach on the last day of school our junior year?" Frankie asked him.

He did, vividly. It had been a half-day and she'd driven them both back to his house. She went up to change and he waited in his living room, nervous and jittery. When she came down stairs, he felt his mouth run dry. It was his first time seeing Frankie in anything less than her usual conservative T-shirts and shorts and there she was, creamy, pale flesh contained in a simple, pink bikini.

"Do you like it?" she'd asked him.

Evan could only nod.

Frankie pulled her jean shorts on over her bikini bottoms and the two walked up to the beach near Evan's house. Evan, admittedly meek and mild-mannered, mustered up the courage to take her hand in his. He was elated when Frankie's reaction was a simple smile. They walked the rest of the way hand-in-hand.

The time they actually spent at the beach was a blur. All he remembered was being unable to take his eyes off of her. He'd heard that high school love wasn't real love, but he'd never, ever felt that way about another girl. It had only been a few years since graduation, but he knew that his heart would always belong to Frankie Noonan.

169

It was dusk by the time they left the beach, walking back down the steep road to his house hand-in-hand. A car with one headlight out drove by and Evan said "Padiddle!"

"What's a Padiddle?" Frankie asked.

Evan explained the rules to her. If a car with one headlight out drove by, the first person to call out 'Padiddle!' got to either slug the other people in the group in the arm or kiss them. He didn't remember where he learned it, but it seemed like an excellent opportunity to steal a kiss from Frankie.

"So which one is it going to be, then?" she asked.

Evan smiled at her, leaned in, and kissed her on the lips. It was quick and painless but when he pulled away, he saw that she was blushing. She didn't say anything and neither did he. Frankie simply took his hand in hers and they continued their way back to his house, where they played video games for another couple hours before she left.

It was the only time he would kiss her. Later that summer, Scott Nutterman asked her out and the two dated all through senior year and Scott asked her to marry him in front of the Magic Kingdom on their class trip to Florida in front of the entire class. Just a few months later and she was dead on impact. A month after that, Evan stepped onto the bus to boot camp.

"It's, it's real nice to see you, Frankie," he told the apparition that floated in front of him.

She smiled. "*It's nice to see you too, Evan.*"

Evan smiled. Part of him wondered if maybe he'd suffered a psychological break and she was a hallucination. Considering the day he was having, the odds were fifty-fifty.

170

"What are you doing here?" he asked her.

"I need you to do something for me, Evan. I need you to save the world."

The odds of him being crazy increased to sixty-forty. "H-how am I supposed to do that?"

"There is an item of great magical power in this place called the Wellspring. It is what the Lich is after. It must be destroyed. If he were to get his hands on it, all of reality would be at risk."

Evan looked at Frankie's ghost. "How am I supposed to destroy such a powerful item?"

The translucent blue vision of the love of his life looked at the rifle. *"Weren't you the best shot in Basic Training?"*

Evan had indeed been the best shot, but how did she know that? She'd already died before he'd ever held his first gun.

"Evan, please, we're running out of time!" Frankie said, a sudden urgency in her voice. *"Destroy the Wellspring. Be the hero you were meant to be!"*

He stood. Frankie's ghost smiled and put a hand to his cheek. It tingled, sort of like VapoRub.

Suddenly, Evan felt a lot braver. He returned the ghost's smile. "I guess I'll go save the world then."

"Thank you, Evan."

Evan made his way down the hall, then felt compelled to tell Frankie the one thing he'd never gotten to tell her when she was alive.

171

"Frankie, I love-"

To his dismay, the apparition was gone. But it didn't matter. He had a job to do.

VII.

The Lich grinned as the Lenoir girl finally showed her face. The two men that had caused him such a headache were with her. *Three harpies, one stone,* he thought to himself with a grin. The Wellspring was so close it took all of his willpower to not run right towards the younger, fitter man that had it on his person and tear it from him and then divorce him from his innards. Sheer force of will won the day and the Lich was able to keep his cool.

The zombies made their way towards the trio, but the Lich issued them a command to hold. All at once they all froze in place, a mass of fleshy statues.

"Little Marjorie, I've been waiting for you," he said. "I believe you and your friends have something of mine."

The girl smirked. "The only thing we have for you is the True Death, monster."

And with that, she launched a bolt of lightning at him. He used Deathbringer like a lightning rod and the bolt simply fed the ravenous staff's endless hunger.

"Come now," the Lich said, chuckling. "You'll need more than those little parlor tricks to-"

A fireball hit him in the face.

"Oh, you little-"

She began to throw every spell in the book at him. The Lich made a mental note to have the skeletons do a better job of hiding those spell book pages next time a monster hunter decided to challenge him.

In addition to fireballs, lightning bolts, phantom blades, light beams, and all the other attack spells the girl had added to her repertoire, both men were shooting at him.

"I'VE HAD JUST ABOUT ENOUGH OF YOU!" the Lich bellowed. He released his hold on the zombies and they made a beeline for the trio of gnats who had dared to be so bold as to stand up to the mighty Lich.

"Hey, ugly!" the man with the Wellspring called out.

The Lich turned his attention to the man and for the first time in decades, he found himself experiencing something resembling fear.

The man held his blunderbuss to the Wellspring. Again, the zombies froze.

"Now, let's not be hasty..." the Lich began.

But before he could continue, a small girl ran out into the courtyard.

"Daddy!" she cried.

The man with the Wellspring turned and looked at the girl. "Junebug?"

The Lich grinned. What delightful timing. He darted over and snatched the girl up. She screamed.

"LET HER GO!" the man cried, his voice dripping with desperation.

"DADDY!" the girl, 'June,' squealed.

He had the man right where he wanted him. A sense of tranquility settled over the Lich. It truly *was* his destiny to ascend to godhood. Despite the minor inconveniences he'd faced over the course of his siege on the pentagonally-shaped stronghold, his unholy quest was nearly complete.

174

"Give me what is mine and I will give you what is yours," he said, his growing ever-larger.

"Jefferson, don't!" the Lenoir girl warned.

"I hate to say it but I'm with the lady, kid," the other man said.

"Tick-tock, tick-tock, will this little piggy join my flock?" the Lich taunted.

The child's father looked at his compatriots and shook his head. "I'm sorry. She's my whole world. I have to do this."

As the man made his way across the courtyard, the Lich couldn't help but feel bats in his stomach from the giddy excitement he was experiencing.

Victory was at hand at last.

VIII.

Alex was frozen in place as she watched the events unfolding in front of her. Not only had she failed in her job of keeping June safe, but because of her inability to perform that one simple task, the Big Bad was going to win.

She was a failure. How was she supposed to live with herself with whatever time she had left? She may as well have gift-wrapped June and handed the girl to the Lich herself.

Movement across the courtyard caught her eye: a young soldier stood in the entrance of the café holding what looked to be some sort of laser gun.

She looked back to the portal, where the Lich stood. Jefferson was handing him a crystal ball that appeared to be filled with smoke and a soothing golden light. It was...*beautiful*. Marjorie and Jack Manning both watched in horror as the Lich took the crystal ball from Jefferson. He held it above his head and cackled loud enough that Alex could hear it ringing in her ears. A fleeting thought about how he sounded a lot like Skeletor drifted through her mind before being drowned out by the sheer terror of the situation.

Turning her gaze back to the soldier, she watched as he took aim and squeezed the trigger. A pulse of purple energy zipped across the courtyard battlefield and hit its mark.

The crystal ball shattered, sending a gold-tinged shockwave outward that caused all of the zombies to return to their natural postmortem state and an impossible amount of fluffy, light gray smoke began to fill the area and drift upward and away from the Pentagon.

"NO!" the Lich screamed. "*NO!* I was so close."

Alex watched as he dropped June and turned his attention to the source of the ball's destruction.

"YOU!" he screeched, pointing a bony finger at the soldier.

To Alex's amazement, the soldier was smiling.

The smile remained even as the monstrous necromancer bound towards the young man.

IX.

Even as the Lich lifted him off the ground and roared in his face, Evan couldn't help but smile. He had done it. He'd destroyed the Wellspring and saved the world. Maybe even more than just the one.

Closing his eyes, he prepared himself for whatever came next, and then, for what came after that.

His teeth gritted together as the necromancer tore his stomach open, but the pain disappeared quickly, replaced by a tingly feeling just like VapoRub on his lips.

"*Thank you, Evan,*" Frankie's voice whispered.

And still, as the Lich continued to unravel him, Evan Clark smiled.

X.

June clung to her father for dear life and he clung right back to her.

She had been so scared. The monster, who smelled like someone had left a pile of expired meat in her grandmother's closet for a month, had almost killed her. Even in her terrified state, June found herself taking pride in that she didn't even wet her pants.

Head buried against her father's muscular leg, the girl could hear Jack ask, "Plan B?" She didn't know what it meant, but her father replied with, "Yeah, Plan B."

"It was nice knowing you, Brody. I'll send that postcard once I get settled in."

"Good luck, Gramps."

"And, uh, one last thing," Jack said to her father.

June pulled away just in time to see Jack slip her father a folded up piece of paper. He looked at her, smiled, ruffled her hair, and then turned and ran towards the giant portal in the middle of the courtyard. She looked up at her father.

"Where's he going, Daddy?"

Her father smiled. "He's going to save the day."

XI.

Jack ran. He ran faster and harder than he had in ten, hell, twenty years. The Lich was distracted courtesy of his rage fugue and the poor kid who caused it was bearing the brunt of the necromancer's tantrum. Jack didn't have time to see how bad it was, however. He had a job to do.

"When you cross the threshold into the Lich's inner sanctum, the first thing you'll want to do is see if you can find a power source for the portal," a voice said. Jack realized it was from the sword Marjorie had given him.

"Sounds simple enough," he replied, feeling a little silly in spite of the chaos surrounding him.

He reached the portal and without a second thought, ran through it and into the realm of Arcania.

The Lich's inner sanctum looked like a used book store from the Dark Ages. Stacks of books on top of stacks of books and all kinds of other knick-knacks strewn about. Jack looked all over for some sort of magic gem or contraption or any sort of magical fantasy bullshit that was keeping the portal open.

"There's nothing here," he told the sword.

"Is there some sort of collection of runes or sigils on the floor?"

Jack looked down, and sure enough, the portal was in the center of an elaborate circle full of arcane symbols. "Yeah, a whole bunch of them."

"Find a way to deface them. Disrupt the circle and the portal will close."

Jack looked around for something, anything, that would get the job done and saw a bell jar that had some sort of pickled vegetable monster inside of it. He grabbed it and dumped the puke-green liquid on top of the circle. The portal flickered as the liquid spread across the circle. Jack ripped off his filthy shirt and dropped to his knees. He ran it across some of the runes and they smudged. Just like that, the portal was gone.

Jack sat down on the ground, grunting as the weird pickle-like juice soaked his pants, and let out a long, deep sigh of relief. "It's done."

"*Well met, friend,*" the sword told him. "*I think this is the beginning of a beautiful relationship.*"

Jack, suddenly gobsmacked with just how physically exhausted he was, grinned. "Just don't call me Gramps and we'll get along just fine." He looked around the Lich's sanctum. "Now what?"

"*Well, I suppose that's really up to you.*"

XII.

The Wellspring had been destroyed and magic had been released into a mundane realm. It was not ideal by any stretch of the imagination, but at least it meant that the Lich's plan had been foiled. Marjorie saw Jack head toward the portal and knew that she had to do whatever she could to keep the Lich distracted.

Marjorie ran at the Lich, white-knuckling the Reaper's Scythe. The monster was in the midst of relieving the man who destroyed the Wellspring of his internal organs. Charging up her attack, which caused her to pulse ever-so-slightly with a golden light, the last Lenoir leapt into the air and brought the scythe down on the Lich's arm. He roared in pain, dropped the poor, disemboweled man and turned his attention to her.

Marjorie gripped the scythe and grinned. "It's the final boss battle, Lich. It ends here."

"It is certainly the end for one of us, I assure you," he growled.

With alarming speed, he grabbed her by the neck and lifted her off the ground much like he had with the soldier that was dying beside them.

The Lich pulled her in close. "I'm going to take you apart piece by piece, little girl. You'll beg for death but all you will know is mind-searing agony until, days from now, I finally grant you that sweet, sweet release."

Marjorie smiled.

The Lich snarled. "What could you *possibly* be smiling about?"

"I have a good feeling that my distraction worked like a charm."

"Distraction?"

Marjorie heard a sound like all the air being sucked out of a room from behind her as the portal to Arcania closed.

"No," the Lich said, his voice devoid of any particular emotion. Then, his body deteriorated and Marjorie found herself on the ground next to a pile of bones and ash.

Just like that, it was over. The Lich was dead. Her family had been avenged. She didn't know whether to laugh or cry so she did both.

It wasn't until she heard a meek voice off to her side saying something that Marjorie remembered the dying soldier.

She crawled over to him. "It's okay. I'm here with you."

"I...I did it, didn't I?" he asked her. "I saved the day."

Marjorie smiled and nodded, lying to the man. "You sure did." Then, she followed it with the truth. "Because of you, we were able to send someone across to my realm to disrupt the portal."

The man smiled back and then coughed up blood. "I'm dying."

Marjorie took his hand and nodded. "I wish I had a Potion or Elixir to give you," she said, regretting her poor inventory management in the hours leading up to crossing through the portal.

"It's okay. Now I get to see Frankie."

She didn't know who Frankie was, she didn't even know who the dying man was, but she nodded all the same. "What's your name, friend?"

"Evan. Evan Clark, Private first class."

"Well, Evan Clark," Marjorie said, squeezing his hand, "when you see Frankie, you say hi for me, okay?"

He nodded. "I-I will. You tell Nutterbutter for me that he's a, he's a..." Then, Evan Clark gave her a quizzical look, as if he lost his train of thought, and then he was gone. She closed his eyes and wept.

Moments later, Marjorie felt small arms around her. It was June.

"Thank you," the girl told her.

Marjorie reached a hand up and placed it on the girl's head. "You're welcome, dear."

She got to her feet and looked at her comrade-in-arms, Jefferson Brody. "We did it."

"Yeah, I guess we did," he said, tears staining his cheek.

Then, Alex joined them. Marjorie was very glad that she appeared largely unharmed.

"I'm sorry I let June get into danger," the woman told Jefferson.

He threw his arm around her in a sort of side-hug Marjorie had never seen before. "Hey, it's cool! No harm done. Thank you for taking care of her."

"Can you guys stop talking about me like I'm not right here?" June asked.

At this, Jefferson and Alex both laughed. Marjorie smiled. She still couldn't believe it was all over.

"Dad?"

"Yes, Junebug?"

"Can we get some frozen yogurt?"

Jefferson smiled. "Now *that* is an excellent idea."

Marjorie had no clue what 'frozen yogurt' was, but something told her that it was something to look forward to, the first of many things she would discover in this new realm.

With one last glance at the pile of dust and bones that had been the dreaded necromancer that had slain her entire family, Marjorie followed her new friends as they made their way back inside the fortress.

Epilogue:
Two Weeks Later

I.

A lot can happen in fourteen days.

In the two weeks that followed the fall of the Lich and the release of magic into our mundane world, many things had changed.

These are but a sliver of those things.

In Palo Alto, California, a ten-year-old boy named Andrew discovered that his mood determined the local weather. When he was happy, the sun shined and there wasn't a cloud in the sky. When he was sad, it rained and rained. That his parents were in the midst of an ugly, *ugly* divorce meant that, for at least the city of Palo Alto, the California Drought was over.

A first-generation German immigrant named Karl living in London, England, had been haunted by terrifying visions of a future apocalypse. His son and daughter-in-law, both too busy to deal with what they assumed was dementia, had the man committed to the Bethlem Royal Hospital. While there, his psychiatrist, Doctor Lara Sanders, became obsessed with the old man's dream journal and began to study it like a woman possessed.

Doctors were baffled when a Topeka woman brought her five-year-old son, Ralphie, to the hospital due to what appeared to be an overnight case of progeria. The once-youthful boy looked like he'd aged seventy years, looking like a little old crone instead of the bright, bubbly boy that would be attending kindergarten in the fall. As the radiology department at Saint Francis was not equipped to scan for magical parasites, they would miss the snot-like creature that had wrapped itself around young Ralphie's spinal column as it slowly began to exert control over the boy. The parasite, known to the people of Arcania as a Babayog, used children as hosts, contorting their bodies and leeching their youth until they were weak enough to use as a vessel to spread magical mischief across the land.

In the middle of her Film Studies class at the University of Houston, a senior named Amy majoring in film history had a seizure and began speaking in tongues during a viewing of Hitchcock's *Rope*. Another student in her class recorded the event and sent it to a family friend who worked as a linguistics professor by the name of Peter Sprang at Miskatonic University in Massachusetts, who almost immediately recognized it as ancient Macedonian. The outburst loosely translated to "Hell will freeze over. The sky will fall. The Titans will be freed." Now, if Sprang were to pass that information on to a particular psychiatrist in London, puzzle pieces would fall into place, but it would still be some time before either one would know of the other's existence. As a postscript on this particular incident, it should come as no surprise that poor Amy has no memory of the event.

A farmer named Marshall in Hillsville, Virginia discovered that he had mandrakes growing in his garden. Unfortunately for Marshall, this discovery proved to be fatal as the first mandrake he pulled up emitted a scream that caused a cerebral hemorrhage, killing the farmer instantly.

One state over in nearby Mason County, two teenagers and life-long best friends named Rusty and Becka went looking for the legendary Mothman in the McClintic Wildlife Management Area. They stumbled upon an old munitions building and, lacking the common sense that came with age, opened the ancient, rusty door and went inside. While they did not find the Mothman, the friends did discover what appeared to be a skinless dog that stood upright had made its home in the building. It giggled like a little girl as it fell upon them. Neither lived to tell the tale, although something wearing Becka's face did return home that evening to two very relieved parents. So relieved, in fact, that neither one thought it odd that Becka's boisterous, hearty laugh had been replaced with a shrill, child-like giggle.

In Seoul, South Korea, a young girl named Ji-min opened up her closet to discover a family of faeries had made their nest out of one of her favorite shirts. She assured the little, winged creatures that she would keep them a secret.

Back in our familiar setting of Washington, D.C., two particular instances occurred worth noting:

A young soldier who had given his life to help stop an undead necromancer from using a magical artifact to become a dark god found himself, rather unexpectedly, back in the land of the living. He was still technically quite dead, but it would appear that fate had other plans in store for him. He found himself suddenly very much awake and aware in the coffin-like morgue drawer his body had been placed in. The door to the drawer was opened and the slab he was on was pulled out and, very much to his surprise, the ghost of the general he'd fought alongside floated there. Despite being pulled from the afterlife, from the girl he loved, the soldier couldn't help but smile when the ghost general told him that they still had that beer to get to.

189

For an eleven-year-old girl that had been through the ordeal that she had gone through, June Brody seemed largely unfazed. While she didn't know all the details due to the novel-sized NDA's her ex-husband had been forced to sign, Frannie Covington knew her daughter had been through a fairly harrowing experience during her visit to the Pentagon and compared to some of the horror stories she'd heard about the after-effects some children experienced, she didn't think it strange at all that her daughter had developed a new imaginary friend. However, she wasn't crazy about the name that June had chosen. Something about 'Gorden Nightshade' just didn't sit right with her.

II.

The memorial service was a farce. Jefferson, Alex, Marjorie and the other survivors of the Lich's attack on the Pentagon had been forced to take part in a rather complex cover-up. Surprising nobody, the government called it a terrorist attack, citing that somehow ISIS or al-Qaeda or whatever Middle Eastern boogeyman of the week Fox News told people to be afraid of had found out about the anti-terrorism training that would leave the Pentagon with a skeleton crew of soldiers to defend it and chose to attack. All of the survivors had been pressured into signing non-disclosure agreements promising their silence or face treason of all goddamn things. The government didn't even seem to care that Marjorie wasn't even from the same dimension, for Pete's sake.

When Senator Powers asked Jefferson if he'd be interested in a spot at the Department of Immigration Studies, he told her that he would be indeed. He hadn't been back to work since the 'terrorist attack' had occurred and the thought of not having to return to the Pentagon certainly seemed relevant to his interests, *especially* without Jack to tease for eight hours a day. When he found out that she'd offered Alex and Marjorie jobs as well, that only sweetened the deal.

After everything that had happened, Jefferson felt like a new man. The slutty bachelor who spent his freetime at the bar and took home a different girl every night no longer existed. In his stead was a more mature man who was ready to work on improving himself and his life, including beginning the discussion with Frannie over readjusting their custody arrangement. June was the single most important thing in his life and he almost lost her. Only getting her on the weekends, especially when he hadn't done anything wrong in the first place, was no longer tenable. Frannie knew that he and their daughter had been through hell and she knew that he had gone to great lengths to protect June, so Jefferson was optimistic that she would be agreeable.

Standing in the corner of the reception hall after the memorial service, drinking a cranberry juice and seltzer, Jefferson thought about how the world had changed. News headlines started to sound more and more like the sort of stories you'd see on the cover of *Weekly World News*. Stuff like that poor kid in Kansas who looked like he'd turned 80 overnight seemed so surreal to him. He had been there, at Ground Zero (literally), when magic had been released into the world. Every sighting of a werewolf or vampire or Sasquatch, the sort of thing he used to laugh about, suddenly had a lot more credence. Hell, people will be asking each other "Where were you when you heard Dottie the Cow sing 'Hallelujah?'" in ten years.

Jefferson was stirred from his thoughts when he heard someone call his name. He looked up to see Alex walking up to him. She looked great in her black blouse and skirt and white, fuzzy cardigan.

She greeted him with a 1000-watt smile and wrapped him in a big hug. "Hey stranger, wasn't sure if I'd see you here or not," she said as she pulled away.

Jefferson shrugged. "I needed time. With everything that's gone on, it's...it's a lot to take in." He took a sip of his drink. "I mean, we're two of the only people in this room that know that there's other worlds out there, that there's *literally* magic in the air, and we can't say boo about it. Channing Tatum or Wes Bentley won't ever portray Jefferson Brody in the Michael Bay production of *Black Friday: Ride of the Valkyrie*." At that, Alex laughed. "I just have a lot of feelings right now. I'm all mixed up."

Alex took Jefferson's hand in hers. "I know how you feel. But what matters is that we are still here. The best thing we can do is live our lives. We can't let this tragedy define us."

He grinned. "Are you just vomiting snippets of *Human Resources 101* at me now?"

Alex snorted. Jefferson had never heard her do that before. "You're on to me." She smiled again. "I'm sorry, I've had a few drinks. Liquid courage. You know."

"What do you need liquid courage for?"

Rolling her eyes, Alex asked him, "Have you not been reading my texts? I'm taking Marjorie out on a date tonight."

This took Jefferson by surprise. "Oh yeah?"

Alex nodded. "Yeah. I figured, hell, I almost died two weeks ago, maybe I should start putting myself out there. I mean, I'm young and smart and talented and I deserve a totally hot babe from another world that can shoot lightning out of her fingers to come home to, y'know?"

"She asked you, didn't she?"

Alex finished her drink. "Oh, yeah, definitely. I'm pretty sure June had something to do with it to be quite honest."

Jefferson smiled. Alex's hypothesis was more than likely right on the money. June had told him on several occasions that she thought the two women would be a cute couple and, like her mother, she loved playing cupid.

"Oh, shoot, speaking of the date, I've got to go get ready! Pretty sure that in any dimension, funeral outfits should never double as date attire."

"Do you need a ride? I don't think you should be driving."

She waved a hand at him. "Nah, I got an Uber. Don't you worry about me, Mr. Man." She hugged him again. "I'll see you tomorrow, huh? Big first day!"

"Yeah, I'll see you tomorrow. Good luck tonight. Tell Marj I said hi."

Alex nodded. "I will! Give Junebug a kiss for me."

Then, she was gone, leaving Jefferson alone again. He looked at his cell phone. It was almost 5:00. He'd spent plenty of time going through the motions. It was time to go. He figured he'd swing by Frannie's to see June and play catch or something in the backyard and then call it an early night. Orientation for the DIS began at 8:30 AM and the All-New, All-Different Jefferson Brody planned on showing up bright-eyed and bushy-tailed.

As he walked out to his car, Jefferson thought about Jack and the note that the older man had given him before going through the portal. It was just two simple words, but it spoke volumes: 'Stop RGS.' It was certainly a tall order, but Jefferson felt like he had to at least try. Jack had saved the day in the end, closing the portal and cutting the Lich off from his phylactery. Picking up where he had left off with Roosevelt Globl was the least that Jefferson could do. Pulling out of the reception hall's parking lot, he hoped that, if nothing else, the old man was happy.

III.

Jack Manning hadn't been anything resembling 'happy' in months but after two weeks in the realm of Arcania, he was certainly on his way. It was a realm of magic and wonders, where an old guy with a magic, talking sword could be a real hero. There were no superiors telling him that he couldn't go and root out that den of werebears that were terrorizing the nearby hamlet and no evil corporations using their limitless funds to run the world from behind the scenes. There was just Good and Evil and Jack found that with every zombie or giant spider or golem he decapitated, he felt that much better.

"Be careful, Jack," d'Argetan cautioned as he entered the dank cave. *"Mermen are weak on their own, but they live in clusters. Don't let yourself be overwhelmed."*

"Yeah, yeah, yeah. I can handle a few walking fish sticks, or have you forgotten that I took out the 'fearsome Frost Juggernaut' without a single fire spell?"

"I still don't understand why you insisted on doing it the hard way," the sword retorted.

Jack smiled as he went deeper into the cave. "The hard way builds character."

"I do suppose you're right, although I'm not positive that you gained any additional experience for doing it the hard way."

Pulling a torch out of his bag of holding, Jack lit it with a small burst of flame from his finger. "Nothin' personal, d'Argetan, but it's awfully hard to be careful and conscious of my surroundings when the disembodied voice of a two-hundred-year-old monster hunter nagging me about my methods of killing giant frozen constructs left behind by some ancient wizard."

No response from the sword.

"S'what I thought," Jack muttered to himself.

As he continued deeper into the cave, the sound of running water could be heard. He was getting close. Three days ago, Jack had taken a job from the bounty board in the little fishing village of Damus in Eastern Arcania. Their farm animals had been savaged several nights in a row and according to d'Argetan, the evidence pointed to mermen. Jack asked around and the old man at the item shop pointed him in the direction of Damus Lake. Low and behold, there was a cave. If the mermen had set up a nest anywhere, it would be in the dark, dank depths within.

Jack was a born warrior. His whole life, he had to curb his natural aptitude with weaponry and tactics, always had someone above him telling him that he had to play by the rules, toe the line, SOP, all that bullshit. Now, in this new world, he could save lives by swinging a sword. He could end reigns of terror with a well-placed magic missile. After two weeks of monster hunting, Jack Manning was full of confidence and a little thing like a merman infestation was already small potatoes to him.

But you know what they say about hubris.

The narrow path he'd been following opened up into a giant cavern. The carcasses of assorted animals were scattered about. Brightly colored fishmen munched away at pieces of cow or chicken, too busy to notice that they had an intruder.

"*Remember, Jack-*" d'Argetan began.

"Weak alone, tough in a cluster. Stop nagging."

Jack ran through a checklist of the spells he'd learned over the past two weeks, trying to find which would be most fun for him. He settled on one of his favorites.

"Hey, fishface!" he shouted to the nearest merman. The monsters all turned and looked at him, then hissed when they saw him standing there. Jack flung out his right arm and unleashed an Unkindness of Ravens. A mess of ravens materialized out of thin air, flying straight for the merman. They did exactly what Jack had hoped they would and tore into the bright red monster.

"Not exactly my first choice for a spell, but effective nonetheless."

Jack grinned as the sea monsters charged him. He charged right back and began to slice through them with Finem. It was like filleting fish. By the time he realized he was drastically outnumbered, it was far too late. The mermen were upon him, taking him down to the ground, piranha-like teeth gnashing in his face. His mana was too low to create a Shock Barrier and there were just too many of them to escape. But Jack Manning was not going to leave the land of the living at the slimy hands of a bunch of overgrown fish sticks, no sir. He pursed his lips and made a shrill whistle, then prepared himself for some pain.

Seconds later, he gritted his teeth as an immense shock coursed through his body as he and the pile of mermen were all hit with a few hundred volts of electricity. While not dead outright, the mermen were certainly well on their way, giving him an opportunity to get out from under them.

Looking over at the entrance to the cavern, Jack saw his new partner standing there, already nocking another arrow. Hess, the only name she'd given him when they'd first met, was an arrowcaster, some sort of hybrid wizard-archer thing. She could fill her glass arrowheads with spell energy and then, after loosing the arrow, it would release the spell on impact.

"Hope you saved your appetite, old man," Hess called over to him as the tip of her arrow filled with orange-red energy, "because we're having a good ol' fashion fish fry tonight!"

She released the arrow and it sank into the ground in the center of the merman horde, releasing a potent fire spell. Before he knew it, Jack watched as the remaining monsters burned.

Back at their campsite, the two monster hunters feasted on merman by the fire. Jack was actually surprised at how delicious they were. Tasted kind of like swordfish.

"Do you miss it?" Hess asked him, her mouth full of food.

The question caught him by surprise. Over the last two weeks, Jack hardly thought about home. Surprising him further was the realization that he hadn't thought about the girls in about as long. He took a deep breath and looked at his considerably younger companion.

"Y'know, I don't," he told her honestly. "There was nothing there for me anymore. My old co-work...my old partner was really the only friend I had there, and you remind me a lot of him."

The girl tilted her head. "Yeah? How so?"

"Young, driven, skilled in a fight, and you call me an old man constantly."

Hess grinned. "I just calls 'em as I sees 'em, old man."

Then, the raven-haired girl stood up and stretched. "Well, I'm off to bed. We've got a big day tomorrow. Sneaking into the Graveyard of the Mages and stopping a skeleton uprising before it starts is best done with a full night's rest. G'night."

"Good night, Hess. Thanks for the save earlier."

She shrugged. "I scratch your back, you scratch mine." And with that, she disappeared into her tent.

The incident in the cavern was not the first time Hess had pulled Jack's ass out of the fire. Several days after he had ended up in Arcania, he had taken on his first quest from a bounty board: wipe out a clan of vampires. He thought it would be easy but they proved to have a few hundred years more experience than he had apiece and if it hadn't been for Hess's timely intervention and a quiver full of flame arrows, Jack's brief stint as a monster hunter would have ended before it could even began.

As the abandoned church the vampires had made their home in burned to the ground, Hess introduced herself. After telling her his story, the plucky young girl decided that the 'old man' needed someone to show him the ropes. They'd been inseparable ever since.

It was nice having Hess around. As experienced in the art of slaying monsters as d'Argetan was, a century or two living in a sword hadn't done wonders for his social skills. Beyond the social aspect, Hess's presence was...comforting. Since she had Jack thinking about his old life, he realized how much he'd missed being a dad and watching over someone. Despite her skill as an arrowcaster and bubbly personality, Jack knew that Hess was as tired of being alone in the world as he was, and he was delighted to have her company.

After extinguishing the campfire, Jack crawled into his own tent and quickly fell asleep, a smile on his face.

He might not qualify as 'happy' just yet, but Jack Manning was damn sure on his way.

IV.

As she stood outside of the movie theater, Alex reflected on the fact that she could not remember the last time she wore a dress by choice. The one she was wearing was pistachio green and had a much lower cut (re: any cut at all) than she was used to. But when she looked at herself in the mirror earlier that evening before leaving her apartment, she had to admit that she looked *hot*.

Still, hot or not, the woman felt very anxious. It was her first date with Marjorie and she had no idea what to expect. Marjorie had asked her, via text of all things, if she would like to go on a date two nights earlier. Alex practically launched her phone across the living room when she read the text out of pure shock. After composing herself, she replied in the affirmative and they made their plans.

Meatstadon wouldn't even merit a footnote in the annals of cinematic history but Alex thought, given Marjorie's previous occupation as a monster slayer, that the woman would enjoy spending two hours watching a mastodon-shaped meat monster chase around a bunch of college kids in Alaska.

At least, that was what she was hoping.

"Hi," a soft voice said from behind her.

Alex turned and was taken aback by the vision in red that stood before her. Marjorie, already beyond naturally beautiful, had managed to improve on perfection with some mascara and lipstick and wrapped up her slender, toned body in a crimson red dress.

"You...wow. Hi," Alex said, feeling the blood rush to her cheeks.

Marjorie smiled and tucked a loose strand of fire-red hair behind an ear. "Do you like it? June showed me how to use the YouTube and I watched some videos on how to do make-up."

Alex nodded, but her words failed her.

"Shall we go inside?" Marjorie asked her.

Another nod.

But before they could enter the theater, people came running out of the restaurant across the street, screaming.

Marjorie grabbed one of the people, a ghost-white blond woman. "What is it? What's wrong?"

"Th-the water. It came to life and started attacking people!" The woman wrenched out of Marjorie's grasp and continued to flee in terror.

"Water nymphs," she said. Then, she looked at Alex. "I should go and handle this. I am sorry."

Alex tried to hide her disappointment behind a smile. "It's okay. Go do the hero thing."

Then, much to her surprise, Marjorie leaned in and kissed her. It only lasted a moment, but to Alex, entire universes could've been born in that time. Pulling away, Marjorie told her, "You look very beautiful tonight. I will see you tomorrow."

Once again, Alex could only nod.

As she watched Marjorie take off the heels she'd been wearing to run across the street to deal with some water nymphs, Alex smiled and touched her lips.

Best date ever, she thought to herself before going into the theater to watch the nonsensical horror film.

V.

Like most nights, Senator Laura Powers was the last one at the Department of Immigration Services. Or so she thought. Returning to her office after doing the usual end-of-the-night checks on the various machines monitoring the walls of reality in the basement, the Senator was alarmed to see a young woman sitting in her office in the chair opposite her desk reading *Marie Claire*. The woman had raven-black hair was dressed in a sharp, midnight blue skirt suit.

"I like your suit. Not so much the breaking and entering."

The woman looked up from her magazine and smiled. "Hello, Senator Powers. I hate to barge in on you like this, but I've spent the past two weeks trying to make an appointment."

The Senator took her seat across from the mystery woman. "Yes, well, I've been very busy ever since the terrorist attack."

"Riiiiiight, 'terrorist attack,'" the woman said, making air quotes. Powers *hated* people who made air quotes.

"Oh, do you know something I don't, young lady?"

The woman sat forward. "No ma'am. I know something you *do*. I know that an undead sorcerer came from another world looking for a magical artifact *you* hid twenty years ago and said artifact ended up destroyed, releasing magic into our world." She paused. "Did I get that all right?"

"Who are you?" the Senator asked, uncharacteristically shaken.

The woman reached into her matching black pocketbook and for a split-second, Powers thought that she was going to execute her. Instead, she simply handed the Senator a business card.

It read: "LAUREN LAWTON, ACQUISITIONS, ROOSEVELT GLOBAL SOLUTIONS."

"Ah," the Senator said. "Now it all makes sense. What can I do for you, Ms. Lawton?"

"Well, Senator, some concerned parties, i.e. the RGS board of directors, think that your department needs a little less autonomy. Someone to answer to, in other words."

Powers smiled, the kind of smile that could curdle milk. It was a smile that she had perfected decades earlier and it had served her well. "And what, pray tell, would the world's most profitable company want with an obscure government body that spends all its time studying immigration statistics?"

Lauren smiled back. "We both know that you study a little more than immigration statistics, Senator."

"I'll admit that I have taken to reading the ingredients on all of the so-called 'organic' snacks I've been buying lately. Other than that, I haven't the foggiest idea as to what you're referring to."

A chuckle. The woman stood. "You're a tough nut, Senator Powers, I'll give you that. But Roosevelt Global excels at cracking the toughest nuts. For example, and of course I'm speaking purely hypothetically, when a CIA agent starts sniffing around places where he shouldn't be, his whole family could wind up murdered by," air quotes again, "'the Triads'. Then that CIA agent ends up ping-ponged lower and lower down the totem pole until they end up running the Twitter feed for the DoD. That would just be tragic, wouldn't it?" Another saccharin smile. "We'll be in touch, Senator."

And just like that, Senator Powers found herself alone again.

She looked at the woman's business card briefly before crumpling it up and throwing it in the garbage can under her desk, then walked over to the nearby end table and poured herself some whiskey. Knocking it back in one swig, she proceeded to throw the snifter at the wall across the room. It shattered.

Pulling out her phone, she dialed Thomas Ulysses. He picked up on the first ring.

"Laura? Is everything okay?"

"We need to talk."

"What's wrong?"

"I just got a visit from a woman from Roosevelt Global Solutions. We're on their radar."

A long pause from the other end of the conversation, and then, one word that spoke volumes:

"Fuck."

VI.

Two weeks felt like it had been an eternity on the one hand, but on the other, it felt like time had flown by.

Marjorie had been set up with a cozy home, an 'apartment' as the people of this realm referred to as, as well as a healthy stipend from the Senator; a thank you for helping save the day. Marjorie tried to tell her that the woman didn't owe her a thing, but the Senator would not hear of it.

Jefferson, June, and Alex were kind enough to help her decorate her new home, introduce her to pizza, and spend hours showing her the many small wonders of the new world she inhabited. To date, her favorite one so far was indoor plumbing. It had been two whole weeks and flushing a toilet or taking a hot bath still had not lost their charm.

When the Senator appeared on her doorstep with an offer of a job, Marjorie wasn't sure. When she told her that Jefferson and Alex had both already accepted and that it would even have a little of the action and adventure Marjorie found herself craving, the monster hunter in her found it impossible to say no.

Accepting that job what led her to standing outside of the Department of Immigration Studies at eight in the morning, a whole half hour before she had been requested to arrive. The man that drove the 'Lyft' that brought her drove like the hounds of hell itself were after him. But she couldn't complain. In fact, Marjorie hoped that in those thirty minutes, her nerves would settle.

If d'Argetan were there, he would tell her there was nothing to be afraid of, to which she would reply that she wasn't afraid, just apprehensive. She smiled at the memory of the scared girl that stood before the gates to the Lich's castle. How far she had come.

"Hey," said a voice.

206

"Hello, Jefferson. Did your Lyft driver get you here early as well?"

Her friend chuckled. "No, I drove myself."

"Oh, how wonderful. You will have to teach me how to command one of these vehicles someday."

"You bet."

They looked at the entrance to the building they stood in front of. It seemed so...plain to Marjorie. What could possibly go on behind those doors that could offer action and adventure?

"Oh, you guys are early too?"

Marjorie smiled when she saw Alex walk up. "Hello, Alex," she said, feeling bashful.

"Hello, Marjorie. How'd the water nymph situation go last night?"

Marjorie shrugged. "They were just confused. I brought them to the water. How was *Meatstadon*?"

"Oh man, you saw *Meatstadon*?" Jefferson said, his face lighting up.

"It was exactly what one would expect from a movie about a sentient, mastodon-shaped pile of meat with a score to settle."

"Ah, so it was awesome, then?"

Alex smiled and it made Marjorie's heart sing. June had told her shortly after the Lich's defeat that Alex liked her and even helped her navigate the treacherous road of 'flirting.' She desperately wanted to kiss the woman again but did not know how she, or Jefferson, would react to such a public display.

"Good, you're all here," Senator Powers said as she walked up to the building. Marjorie thought she looked distressed.

"Are you alright, Senator?" she asked.

"There will be time for girl talk later. We've got to get you three orientated ASAP."

"What's the rush, boss lady?" Jefferson asked.

The woman looked at him with tired eyes. "There may well be a war coming, Mr. Brody, and we're all on the front line." Then, Senator Powers smiled. "Welcome to the Department of Immigration Studies, kiddos. Let's get to work."

VII.

There was a certain art to playing the long game and nobody played that game better than Gorden Nightshade. In the millennia that he had roamed the chronoverse, the thing that called himself Gorden Nightshade had played that game over and over and over again. While he wasn't one to namedrop, a certain baby-faced North Korean supreme leader once described him as "the Johnny Appleseed of evil." Gorden thought that that was not an altogether terrible analogy, but he viewed himself as more of the person who brings the horse to water. It's up to the horse as to whether or not it wanted to drink.

For example, while Gorden may have carefully forged a young boy into one of the most powerful necromancers in his entire realm, it was ultimately that necromancer's decision to invade another dimension in an attempt to seize a ludicrously powerful artifact that would effectively transform him into a god.

But how would that necromancer have found that artifact in the first place if it had been buried deep underground in a room covered in warding spells? Well, if they were to all of a sudden fail one day with seemingly no explanation, there was a very strong possibility that the necromancer could divine the artifact's location and open up a portal to that dimension.

Naturally, this would beg the question: how? Well, that answer is simple. The wards were always meant to fail. Gorden Nightshade simply put on the face of a long-dead warlock and traipsed his way from one realm to the other with artifact in hand, performed a few parlor tricks, and had the so-called Department of Immigration Studies eating out of his hand. Then, it was just a matter of weaving the right spells.

As to how the action would play out after those wards went down, it was anybody's guess. The century that Gorden had spent pruning the apple tree that was Walton Stoneheart was no time at all to a being that had been around since Before. Walton was just one chess piece on one chess board in a room full of chess games in progress. And, as Gorden Nightshade had discovered in his time on that particular Earth, there were ever-so-many pawns just waiting to be placed on new boards.

So Walton had failed to seize supreme power. So what? There were a million realms and a million million Wellsprings. The end result was still perfectly entertaining. There was an overabundance of magic in that world now! The havoc that it was wreaking was absolutely delicious.

Earth, in almost all of its iterations, was a largely mundane place without an outside influence like the destruction of a Wellspring-esque artifact like the Wellspring. It was a place where gods walked amongst those that had long since forgotten them in favor of shows about socialites and videos of people playing video games and screaming at the top of their lungs. A little chaos was exactly what it needed to liven it up.

After the whole incident at the Pentagon had concluded, Gorden was prepared to move on to find the next place to plant his seeds when he noticed something very interesting. The offspring of the big, brave protagonist of that adventure had been right next to the Wellspring when it had detonated, as had her father. Something like that, it marked a person. Gorden decided to wait to go exploring in the ruins of the world next door (the Great Old Ones, his favorite frenemies, had laid waste to it and moved on) in favor of helping the girl discover her true potential.

With nothing but time on his hands, Gorden Nightshade rolled up his sleeves and prepared himself for tea parties and sleepovers.

On the bright side, sticking around meant that he'd have the chance to see how the whole North Korea thing was going to play out...

She was sitting on one of the swings of her wooden swing set, undoubtedly built by her father. The sky was cloudy but the sun was poking through just right as to hide his face in shadow. The girl looked up at him, using her hand to shield her eyes from the light.

"Hello, Junebug," Gorden Nightshade said with a smile.

Not the End.

Acknowledgments

I have a lot of people to thank.

Most importantly I want to thank Shaina, as the title was her idea. If you told me two and a half years ago I'd spin a 200-page novella out of "Mutilated Viking Strippers Take the Pentagon," I'm sure I would not have believed you. Of course, this book wouldn't be a book without a cover, and I am endlessly grateful to my brother Jordan Walsh for the illustrations, my friend Dan James for such an amazing logo, and Nancy Ramos for her tireless efforts in tying it all together. Also very thankful for having Megan Porch draw such a slim, fresh-faced version of me for the author illustration two pages ahead of this one.

As with most of my work, I was very satisfied with myself so I am very thankful for Tim, Adonis, Alyssa, Jazzae', Marissa, Sasha and anybody else who ever spent more than five minutes with the text for their efforts in making it look like I actually know what I'm doing.

My dear friend Saren deserves his own special shout-out for lending me his laptop so I could work on the edits on the final draft, freeing me from the routine of making a two-mile roundtrip to the library on my days off for a scant three hours of potential productivity. He also unlocks a 2x gratitude multiplier for lighting the fire under my butt by telling me he might need his laptop back before going on a two-week trip out of the country. That gave me the motivation I needed to finally finish the job. Thanks, dude.

I would also like to thank author Brian Keene for being accessible enough to respond to his fans via Twitter and subsequently emboldening me to publish this to, in part, get a physical copy into his hands.

I'm especially grateful to be loved by two amazing partners, Rose and Megan, and I don't know what I would do without their endless support.

A big thanks to all the people who help get me through the day-to-day drudgery, especially Chelsea, Lyse, Brianna, Kara, Amy, Helen, Shelby, Rob, Emily, Hannah, Ron, Courtney, Taryn, Honey, Alexandra, Kyle, Jay, Catherine, Garrett, Pat, Tom, Ali, Brittainy, everybody in the Wrong Chat, the CT Heroclix posse, and all the other amazing people I know. If you feel left out, please let me know so I can amend these acknowledgments accordingly.

Lastly, I am thankful to you, yes you, reader. I hope you enjoyed this book as much as I enjoyed writing it.

See you next time.

Sean Walsh
Las Vegas, May 2017

About the Author

Sean Walsh was born in the Lawn and Garden section of a Home Depot and raised on a commune by a group of well-meaning occultists. He eventually left to find his fortune in advertising but gave up on his dream after realizing he couldn't spend all day pensively staring out the window with a tumbler of scotch in his hand. After drifting across the country like Roddy Piper's character in *They Live*, he eventually put down roots in the barren desert wasteland of Las Vegas, where he writes weird fiction and loses more and more of whatever faith he had left in humanity every time somebody calls an Icee a Slurpee.

www.ingramcontent.com/pod-product-compliance
Lightning Source LLC
Chambersburg PA
CBHW061217170626
46809CB00007B/2511